Anonymous

War Lyrics and Songs of the South

Anonymous

War Lyrics and Songs of the South

ISBN/EAN: 9783744784177

Printed in Europe, USA, Canada, Australia, Japan

Cover: Foto ©Andreas Hilbeck / pixelio.de

More available books at **www.hansebooks.com**

WAR LYRICS

AND

SONGS OF THE SOUTH.

LONDON:

POTTISWOODE & CO., PRINTERS, NEW-STREET SQUARE.

1866.

TO THE READER.

For reasons that require no explanation, the present volume has been printed in England, under circumstances that have prevented its receiving that revision in passing through the press which otherwise it would have had. The lenient judgment of the reader is therefore requested for any obscurities arising from errors of transcription or other imperfections in the MSS. from which the work has been printed.

PREFATORY ADDRESS.

A 'FAITHFUL FEW' among the 'honorable women, not a few,' in the Northern and Border States of the late Southern Confederacy, have thrown hastily together this 'Book of Poems,' in the hope that its sale to the charitable may secure a fund for the relief of the crippled and invalid men who fought as soldiers in the war at the South; the impoverished women and children, widows and orphans, as well as those who from 'sorrow, need, sickness, and other adversity,' have lost their health and their *minds*. In this hope is it issued, strengthened by their trust in Him who said, 'The poor ye have always with you.'

CONTENTS.

SONGS OF THE SOUTH, AND OTHER POEMS.

a

War Lyrics.

STONEWALL JACKSON'S GRAVE.

BY MRS. M. J. PRESTON.

A simple sodded mound of earth,
   With not a line above it,
With only daily votive flowers
   To prove that any love it;
The token flag that silently
   Each breeze's visit numbers,
Alone keeps martial ward above
   The hero's dreamless slumbers.

No name? no record?   Ask the world—
   The world has heard his story—
If all its annals can unfold
   A prouder tale of glory!
If ever merely human life
   Hath taught diviner moral;
If ever round a worthier brow
   Was twined a purer laurel?

Humanity's responsive heart
   Concedes his wondrous powers,
And pulses with a tenderness
   Almost akin to ours;
Nay, *not to ours*—for us he poured
   His life—a rich libation—
And on adoring souls *we* bear
   This blood of consecration.

B

A twelvemonth only since his sword
  Went flashing thro' the battle—
A twelvemonth only since his ear
  Heard war's last deadly rattle;
And yet have countless pilgrim feet
  The pilgrim's guerdon paid him,
And weeping women come to see
  The place where they have laid him.

Contending armies* bring in turn
  Their meed of praise or honor,
And Pallas here has paused to bind
  The cypress wreath upon her.
It seems a holy sepulchre,
  Whose sanctities can waken
Alike the love of friend or foe—
  Of Christian or of Pagan !

They come to own his high emprise,
  Who fled in frantic masses
Before the glittering bayonet
  That triumphed at Manassas ;
Who witnessed Kernstown's fearful odds,
  As on their ranks he thundered,
Defiant as the storied Greek
  Amid his brave three hundred !

They will recall the tiger spring,
  The wise retreat—the rally ;
The tireless march, the fierce pursuit
  Through many a mountain valley.
Cross Keys unlock new paths to fame,
  And Port Republic's story
Wrests from his ever-vanquished foes
  Strange tributes to his glory !

* In the month of June 1864 the singular spectacle was pre-
sented at Lexington of two hostile armies in turn reverently
visiting the grave of Stonewall Jackson.

Cold Harbor rises to their view,
 The Cedar's gloom is o'er them,
And Antietam's rough-wooded heights
 Stretch mockingly before them.
The lurid flames of Fredericksburg
 Right grimly they remember,
That lit the frozen night's retreat,
 That wintry-wild December.

The largess of this praise is flung
 With bounty rare and regal;
Is it because the vulture fears
 No longer the dead eagle?
Nay! rather far accept it thus—
 An homage true and tender,
As soldier unto soldier's worth—
 As brave to brave will render!

But who shall weigh the wordless grief
 That leaves in tears its traces,
As round their leader crowd again
 Those bronzed and veteran faces?
The 'old brigade' he loved so well—
 The mountain men who bound him
With bays of their own winning, ere
 A tardier fame had crowned him.

The legions who had seen his glance
 Across the carnage flashing,
And thrilled to catch his ringing 'Charge,'
 Above the volley crashing;
Who oft had watched the lifted hand,
 The inward trust betraying,
And felt their courage grow sublime
 While they beheld him praying.

Good knights and true as ever drew
 Their swords with knightly Roland,
Or died at Sobieski's side
 For love of martyred Poland;

Or knelt with Cromwell's ' Ironsides,'
   Or sung with brave Gustavus,
Or on the field of Austerlitz
   Breathed out their dying ' *Aves* ! '

Rare fame ! rare name ! if chanted praise
   With all the world to listen—
If pride that swells a nation's soul—
   If freemen's tears that glisten—
If pilgrim's shining love—if grief,
   Which naught may soothe or sever—
If *these* can consecrate, this spot
   Is sacred ground for ever !

THE CONFEDERATE PARADOX.

The falling débris now aids in strengthening Fort Sumter.—
Telegram, Charleston, Nov. 6, 1863.

A seeming evil often is
   A great and glorious benefit,—
Apparent good a direful curse
   Seducing us to ruin's pit.
The dread volcano towering high
   Rolls on the fertile plains red fire,—
A great and needful safety-valve,
   Through which as 'twere the burning ire
Of subterranean Titans mad
   Escapes, and thus prevents these grim
Old giants strong from bursting through,
   In their terrific wrathful whim,
Their gloomy dungeon's rock-bound roof,
   And burying in destruction wild,
And raging floods of liquid fire,
   Our Mother-earth and every child.
Old Winter with his head of snow
   We hate, and shun his breath so cold ;
But still, a true physician, he
   Doth make our bodies strong and bold.

Misfortunes, cares, and trials, and woes,
　　But nerve the soul of man at length;
And he who never hath felt such
　　Is weak—he lacks an inward strength.

Old Sumter stands with naked face,
　　His rock-ribbed bosom courts the shot,—
A mighty shield for Liberty,
　　Nor day nor night is she forgot;
And when Hell's engines hurl their bolts,
　　And make him bend his towering form,
He but presents a *double front,*—
　　Doubly defies the infernal storm!
The Yankees and their ally loved,
　　His great Satanic Majesty,
May thunder threaten, curse and yell,
　　Crouched at their feet he'll never be.

'Mid heat of fire and blows of might
　　The iron which on the anvil lies,
But stronger and more solid grows,
　　As sturdy smith his hammer plies.
Then bare your breasts, ye Southern men,
　　Let hate and fate pound as they will,
Trust in your hearts and God who made,—
　　For freedom strike, and strike to kill!

MORGAN'S WAR SONG.

BY GENERAL B. W. DUKE, C. S. A.

Ye sons of the South, take your weapons in hand,
For the foot of the foe hath insulted your land!
　　　Sound, sound the loud alarm!
　　　Arise, arise and arm!
Let the hand of each freeman grasp the sword to
　　maintain
Those rights which, once lost, he can never regain.
Gather fast 'neath our flag, for 'tis God's own decree,
That its folds shall still float o'er a land that is free!

See ye not those strange clouds which now darken
    the sky?
Hear ye not that stern thunder, now bursting so nigh?
        Shout, shout your battle-cry!
        Win, win this fight or die!
To your country devote every life that she gave,
Let the land they invade give their army its grave,
Gather fast 'neath our flag, for 'tis God's own decree,
That its folds shall still float o'er a land that is free!

On our hearts and our cause and our God we rely,
And a nation shall rise or a people shall die,
        Form, form the serried line—
        Advance our proud ensign;
What our fathers achieved our own valor can keep,
And we'll save our fair land, or we'll sleep our last
    sleep.
Gather fast 'neath our flag, for 'tis God's own decree,
That its folds shall still float o'er a land that is free!

Tho' their plunder-paid hordes come to ravish our
    land,
Give our fields to the spoiler, our homes to the brand,
        Our souls are all aglow
        To face the hireling foe:
Give the robbers to know that we never will yield,
While the arm of one Southron a weapon can wield.
Gather fast 'neath our flag, for 'tis God's own decree,
That its folds shall still float o'er a land that is free!

From our far Southern shore now arises a prayer—
The cry of our women fills with anguish the air;
        Oh! list that pleading voice!
        Each youth now make his choice—
Now tamely submit, like a coward and slave,
Or rise and resist like the free and the brave!
Gather fast 'neath our flag, for 'tis God's own decree,
That its folds shall still float o'er a land that is free!

Kentucky! Kentucky! can you suffer the sight
Of your sisters insulted, your friends in the fight?
      Awake! be free again!
      Oh! break the tyrant's chain!
Seize the sword you once drew but to strike for the
    right,'
From the homes of our fathers drive the dastard in
    flight,
Gather fast 'neath our flag, for 'tis God's own decree,
That its folds shall still float o'er a land that is free!

Knoxville, Tenn.:
  July 4, 1862.

MY LOVE AND I.

BY ASA HARTZ.

My Love reposes on a rosewood frame
      (A 'bunk' have I),
A couch of feathery down fills up the same
      (Mine's straw, cut dry!).
She sinks to sleep at night, with scarce a sigh:
With waking eyes I watch the hours creep by.

My Love her dinner takes in state,
      And so do I (!)
The richest viands flank her silver plate,
      Coarse grub have I!
Pure wines she sips at ease her thirst to slake,
I pump my drink from Erie's limpid lake!

My Love has all the world at will to roam,
      Three acres I!
She goes abroad or quiet sits at home;
      So cannot I!
Bright angels watch around her couch at night,
A Yank, with loaded gun, keeps me in sight.

A thousand weary miles now stretch between
      My Love and I—
To her this wintry night, cold, calm, serene,
      I waft a sigh—
And hope, with all my earnestness of soul,
To-morrow's mail may bring me my parole !

There's hope ahead ! We'll one day meet again,
      My Love and I—
We'll wipe away all tears of sorrow then.
      Her love-lit eye
Will all my many troubles then beguile,
And keep this wayward REB from 'JOHNSON'S ISLE.'

Johnson's Island :
    December 1863.

THE PRISON ON LAKE ERIE.

BY ASA HARTZ.

The full round moon in God's blue bend
    Glides o'er her path so queenly,
Dark shadows creep, fade into light,
    And stars look down serenely ;
A captive looks out on the scene,
    A scene so sad, so dreary,
And thinks a weary captive's thoughts
    In prison on Lake Erie.

The happy, happy days of youth
    Flit by him fast and faster ;
The days which gave no warning note
    Of manhood's dire disaster.
The days when joy and peaceful homes,
    And firesides, bright and cheery,
Come back, to find him sad and worn,
    A prisoner on Lake Erie !

THE PRISON ON LAKE ERIE.

A passing cloud flits o'er the scene;
　The light, a moment banished,
Returns again—but now, alas!
　The vision bright has vanished:
The happy views of childhood gone,
　Leave but a picture dreary
To rest the aching eyes upon—
　The prison on Lake Erie!

How many moons will rise and wane—
　How many months will languish—
Ere Peace, the white-winged angel, comes
　To soothe a people's anguish?
God speed the long'd and pray'd-for day
　When lov'd ones, bright and cheery,
Shall welcome us around the hearth
　From prison on Lake Erie!

Johnson's Island:
　February 1864.

BATTLE OF SHILOH.

Quick the cannon's shot did pour,
Belching death at every roar,
　　Woe irrelievable,
　　Loss irretrievable.
Each the other's life essaying,
Thousands were the thousands slaying;
　　Death inevitable.
O God! look down with pitying eye,
In mercy stay the unnatural cry
For brother's blood.　O God! draw nigh!
　　Slaughter increasing,
　　Numbers decreasing;
When, verily, borne by airs from hell,
O'er hundreds came the fatal shell,
　　And, my hero fell!

Low upon the moor he lay,
O'er his brow the zephyrs play,
 Calmly awaiting,
 With breath abating,
Death—but as a patriot should,
Only as a true soldier could ;
 Victory elating.
Cold was his pale and noble brow,
His faith in God upheld him now.
Only a sigh so very low
 Rippled the zephyr,
 A last sigh to her
He loved so fondly, and so well,
His precious, faithful Isabel,
 Whom he loved so well.

Hoarser grew the cannon's roar,
Deeper, deadlier than before,
 The fight renewing,
 The foe subduing ;
Havoc, havoc, all around,
Patriot's blood bedewed the ground,
 While fear eschewing.
Amid this scene of wild distress,
A flower—child of the wilderness—
With fragrance cheered his loneliness.
 Quietly lying,
 Peacefully dying,
O'er his soul was breathed a sense
Assuaging agony intense—
 God's holy presence !

The startling shout—' Our's the day ! '
Heard the warrior where he lay,
 Fearlessly lying,
 On God relying ;
Knew the work he had begun,
Nobly, bravely, truly done,
 The foe defying.

As glacier, 'neath the sun's bright ray,
So with a smile he passed away.
Now, o'er his soul will ever play
    A smile supernal
    From God Eternal.
Among the myriad martyrs blest
His weary spirit is at rest
    On his Saviour's breast.

Fainter grew the artillery's boom,
Hundreds quailed before their doom.
    Oppressor defeating,
    Cowards retreating;
Shriller rose the cries and groans,
Clearer came the dying moans,
    Mercy entreating.
Quiet my hero lay, calm and at rest,
His wearisome life—a life of unrest—
Is ended.   With arms crossed on breast,
    So sweetly sleeping,
    Reward now reaping,
Beside him watched the tender flower
Which cheered him in that lonely hour—
    That last lonely hour.

Louisville, Kentucky.

THE SENTRY'S CALL.

BY W. L. SIBLEY, PRISONER.

' Half-past ten o'clock, and all is well!'

Silence, deep, profound, mysterious,
  Gains her way with subtle power;
O'er the mind she holds imperious
  Court within this solemn hour;

Where the sable sky is teeming
With her starry courtiers gleaming,
And the vestal moon is beaming—
　　　　　　　There 'tis well.

Silence o'er dark Erie's waters
　Resting in the lambent air :
Silence over prison-quarters—
　Melancholy silence there.
Hark ! the breathless spell is broken !
Shrill the cry by sentry spoken :
What may not those words betoken—
　　　　　　　' All is well ! '

Half-past ten o'clock, is calling ;
　' All is well.'　Ah ! whence that sigh !
Was it grief in cadence falling,
　From some o'ercharged heart close by ?
Like a weary zephyr dying,
Where October leaves are lying,
Yet the sentry is replying—
　　　　　　　' All is well ! '

From yon lighthouse comes a glist'ning,
　Like a ray of hope it seems,
Eager hearts, to false hopes list'ning,
　Hope that only comes in dreams ;
Oh ! that hope of home returning !
Hoping on, and with a burning ;
Feverish fire of ceaseless yearning—
　　　　　　　' All is well ! '

See a bridge of silver glossing
　Spans the bay from shore to shore ;
Eager fancy o'er it crossing,
　Seeks to wander, evermore :

Seeks to stroll 'mid childhood flowers,
'Midst affection's changeless bowers;
Or with love in moonlit hours;
' All is well!'

But the present still intruding,
 With its harsh repulsive truth,
Comes unbidden here, excluding
 Sweetest dreams of buoyant youth;
For the sweetest dreams are fleeting—
Fancy's self is ever cheating,
Still the sentry keeps repeating—
' All is well!'

' All is well!' the prisoner sleeping
 On his bunk so rude and bare,
Sees an angel mother weeping,
 Hears a young wife's pleading prayer.
' All is well,' while hope forsaking,
Leaves behind it only aching!
' All is well,' while hearts are breaking—
' All is well!'

' All is well!' a spirit tiring
 Of its chains will soon be free;
Yes, a captive, now expiring,
 Soon shall find his liberty!
' All is well!' a soul is fleeting—
Angels hover round with greeting—
And the sentry still repeating,
' All is well!'

Johnson's Island, 1865.

CHICAMAUGA.

' The stream of death.'

Chicamauga! Chicamauga!
 O'er thy dark and turbid wave
Rolls the death-cry of the daring,
 Rings the war-shout of the brave;

Round thy shore the red fires flashing,
  Startling shot and screaming shell—
Chicamauga, stream of battle,
  Who thy fearful tale shall tell ?

Olden memories of horror,
  Sown by scourge of deadly plague,
Long hath clothed thy circling forests
  With a terror vast and vague ;
Now to gather fiercer vigour
  From the phantoms grim with gore,
Hurried by war's wilder carnage
  To their graves on thy lone shore.

Long with hearts subdued and saddened,
  As th' oppressor's hosts moved on,
Fell the arms of freedom backward,
  Till our hopes had almost flown ;
Till outspoke stern valor's fiat—
  ' Here th' invading wave shall stay ;
Here shall cease the foe's proud progress ;
  Here be crushed his grand array ! '

Then their eager hearts all throbbing,
  Backward flashed each battle flag
Of the veteran corps of Longstreet,
  And the sturdy troops of Bragg.
Fierce upon the foemen turning,
  All their pent-up wrath breaks out
In the furious battle clangor,
  And the frenzied battle-shout.

Roll thy dark waves, Chicamauga,
  Trembles all thy ghastly shore,
With the rude shock of the onset,
  And the tumult's horrid roar ;
As the Southern battle-giants
  Hurl their bolts of death along,
BRECKINRIDGE, the iron-hearted,
  CHEATHAM, chivalric and strong,

POLK and PRESTON, gallant BUCKNER,
 HILL and HINDMAN, strong in might,
CLEBURNE, flower of manly valor,
 HOOD, the AJAX of the fight,
BENNING, bold and hardy warrior,
 Fearless resolute KERSHAW,
Mingle battle-yell and death-bolt,
 Volley fierce, and wild hurrah!

At the volleys bleed their bodies,
 At the fierce shot shriek their souls,
While the fiery wave of vengeance
 On their quailing column rolls;
And the parched throats of the stricken
 Breathe for air the roaring flame,
Horrors of that hell-fare tasted,
 Who shall ever dare to name!

Borne by those who, stiff and mangled,
 Paid, upon that bloody field,
Direful cringing awe-struck homage
 To the sword our heroes wield;
And who felt, by fiery trial,
 That the men who will be free,
Though in conflict baffled often,
 Ever will unconquered be!

Learned, though long unchecked they spoil us,
 Dealing desolation round,
Marking with the tracks of ruin
 Many a rood of Southern ground.
Yet, whatever course they follow,
 Somewhere in their pathway flows
Dark and deep a Chicamauga,
 Stream of death to Vandal foes!

They have found it darkly flowing
 By Manassas' famous plain,
And by rushing Shenandoah
 Met the tide of woe again;

Chicamauga, now immortal,
    By the long, ensanguined flight;
Rappahannock, glorious river,
    Twice renowned for matchless fight.

Heed the story, dastard spoilers!
    Mark the tale these waters tell!
Ponder well your fearful lesson,
    And the doom that there befell.
Learn to shun the Southern vengeance,
    Sworn upon the votive sword,
' Every stream a Chicamauga
    To the vile invading horde ! '

THE FLAG OF TRUCE.

By JAY W. BEE, P.A.C.S., 2d Ky. Cav., Morgan's command.

Thou beautiful emblem of Peace—
    White sail upon war's bloody sea,
Hope seemeth to take a new lease
    On life, from its perils now free.

And glad, sinking down in relief,
    Mars furleth his standard of red,
Returneth his sword to its sheath,
    When like a snow-drift thou art spread.

And foes, who have just tried to chill
    Each other's warm breast with cold steel,
Shake hands with apparent good-will—
    ' Good morning, sir !—how do you feel ? '

But why in the eye lurketh ire ?
    Why curleth with scorn the red lip ?
It seemeth the heart's hidden fire
    Would burst through that cloak of friendship !

False man ! how in truth dost thou feel ?
  Tell him *so concerned for thy health* :
' I feel I could chill with cold steel
  Thy warm breast in fight, or by stealth ! '

Ah ! angel of peace, can it be
  That some mocking fiend from below
Hath wickedly stolen from thee
  Thy beautiful banner of snow ?

We stand upon Time's beaten shore,
  And anxiously wait there for thee—
Lo ! 'mid the waves' frown and their roar
  A sail upon war's bloody sea !

Good God ! but it waneth—is gone,
  Deceitful and vain phantasy !
Kind Hope, well for us thou wast born,
  Sweet Peace we must wait yet for thee !

Still let not Despair's sable frown,
  Envelope our souls like a pall ;
The golden-winged sunbeams fly down,
  Dispelling the clouds as they fall.

But let us make friends with old Fate,
  And bear his hard blows with a grin,
Get on the blind side of his pate,
  This game in the long run will win.

Johnson's Island, Ohio :
    July 1864.

SOUTHERN WOMEN.

BY JAY W. BEE, P.A.C.S.

God bless our women, brave and true !
  For them stern death we Southrons dare ;
Bright angels in the clouds of blue
  Smile on their sisters here in prayer—

C

E'er brave and true our flag o'erhead,
    E'er brave and true our land o'errun,
E'er brave and true in exile dread,
    The bravest, truest 'neath God's sun !

Johnson's Island, Ohio :
    December 1864.

LINES WRITTEN ON RECEIVING SOME PRESSED LEAVES AND FLOWERS FROM HOME.

BY JAY W. BEE, P.A.C.S.

Bright leaves and flowers from Vernon's bowers,
    Ye call to mind home memories sweet,
Which soothe my hours with gentle powers,
    · As waters cool the pilgrim's feet.
God grant that ere another year,
    Loved ones I'll meet in rapture sweet,
No more to fear in exile drear,
    But rest, as meet, a pilgrim's feet,
My soil unpressed by hostile tread,
    Loved flag, bright sun, good God o'erhead !

Johnson's Island, Ohio :
    October 1864.

ELEGY ON LEAVING HOME.

By Major WEBBER, 2nd Kentucky Cavalry, Morgan's command.

Air—Good-bye.

Farewell ! Farewell ! my fair loved land,
    Where I hoped to live and die ;
I offer thee my parting hand—
    Again must say good-bye.

Farewell! Farewell! bright woods and fields,
    Fond comrades, friends, and kin;
Hark! the cannon loudly peals,
    I must join the battle din.

Farewell! Farewell! my boyhood's home,
    Where in halcyon days gone by,
Thy hills and dales I was wont to roam,
    Beneath love's peaceful sky.

But, alas! that blissful day's gone by,
    With the dulcet peace of years:
To arms! to arms! all patriots fly,
    A newborn nation cheers.

Fair Freedom's temple's rent in twain,
    Columbia's lost its charms;
We must our sacred rights maintain
    By a firm appeal to arms.

A patriot nation, Phœnix-like,
    From the ruined pile has birth;
With her I am resolved to strike
    For all that's dear on earth.

Farewell! Farewell! kind parents, dear,
    Fond sisters, again good bye!
In freedom's cause I do not fear
    To swell the battle-cry.

Weep not to see your brother and son
    In patriot ranks arrayed,
My heart to freedom's cause is won,
    My country's voice obeyed.

The patriot spark in early life
    You implanted in my breast,
Urges me to my country's strife—
    To see her wrongs redressed.

I 'll bare my breast to the battle's storm
    To defend our homes and rights,
While God upholds and nerves my arm
    To win proud freedom's fights.

Let not my parting cause you pain,
    Oh ! wipe away your tears ;
When smiling Peace shall come again,
    I'll come to cheer your years.

Oh ! will you pray that God above
    Defend me in the strife,
And with his kind protecting love
    Preserve and shield my life !

Farewell ! Farewell ! to the sacred spot
    Where my brother's bones repose—
To avenge his death shall be my lot,
    Till life's last chapter close.

December 1862.

EPISTLE TO THE LADIES.

By W. E. M., of Gen. Lee's Army.

Ye Southern maids and ladies fair,
    Of whatsoe'r degree,
A moment stop—a moment spare—
    And listen unto me.

The summer's gone, the frosts have come,
    The winter draweth near,
And still they march to fife and drum—
    Our armies ! do you hear ?

Give heed then to the yarn I spin,
    Who says that it is coarse ?
At your fair feet I lay the sin,
    The thread of my discourse.

To speak of shoes, it boots not here ;
   Our Q. M's, wise and good,
Give cotton calf-skins twice a year
   With soles of cottonwood.

Shoeless we meet the well-shod foe,
   And bootless him despise ;
Sockless we watch, with bleeding toe,
   And him sockdologise !

Perchance our powder giveth out,
   We fight them, then, with rocks ;
With hungry craws we craw-fish not,
   But, then, we miss the socks.

Few are the miseries that we lack,
   And comforts seldom come ;
What have I in my haversack ?
   And what have you at home ?

Fair ladies, then, if nothing loth,
   Bring forth your spinning wheels ;
Knit not your brow—but knit to clothe
   In bliss our blistered heels.

Do not *you* take amiss, dear miss,
   The burden of my yarn ;
Alas ! I know there's many a lass
   That doesn't care a darn.

But you can aid us if you will,
   And heaven will surely bless,
And Foote will vote to foot a bill
   For succouring our distress.

For all the socks the maids have made,
   My thanks, for all the brave ;
And honoured be your pious trade,
   The soldier's sole to save.

THE STARRY CROSS OF THE SUNNY SOUTH.

A VISION.

The great Architect now erects in the skies
A new constellation that dazzles all eyes;
And His herald bids Heaven and Earth come in state,
That this wondrous event they may thus celebrate;
And the vast hosts celestial are marshalled around,
And the South's humble warriors kneel down on the
    ground,
And hear and sing the refrain from the skies—
' Proud death or liberty!'

And Faith, His great mason, as base, plants the rock
Of religion—that firm and that adamant block.
While the war-angel Michael, his mantle of red,
Hangs upon the blue cross as he bows low his head.
' *Hope of Earth!* ' glorious Freedom with gold stars
    prints there,
And her banner of snow, Truth unfurls to the air;
Then loud is heard the refrain from the skies—
' Proud death or liberty!'

And next the archangel his trumpet doth sound,
Bids the universe hear him in silence profound!
' Lo! the *Cross of the South* the Almighty doth raise!
Ah! let no wicked hand dare its fair form efface;
It shall stand till the skies are rolled up like a scroll,
And the mountains and isles from their firm bases
    roll:
They sing, and loud the refrain comes to earth—
' Proud death or liberty!'

But Earth's other nations, scarce trusting their eyes,
Stand off in their envy, or doubt, or surprise ;
And refuse *recognising the finger of God*,
Though the earth and sky shake at the shake of His
    rod ;
Until one more presumptuous, with curse and with
    frown,
Swears aloud that the Cross of the South shall come
    down ;
And rage and yell like the demons of hell—
' Vile death or slavery ! '

But, like the old giants who mountains high piled,
To scale Jove's great towers in ambition wild ;
So these impious fanatical hordes shall low fall,
And be wrapped in destruction's black terrible pall,
As the great star-eyed Cross stretches out his strong
    arms,
To protect our brave people from dangers and harms.
Then shout, ye free, the refrain from the skies—
' Proud death or liberty ! '

STONEWALL JACKSON'S WAY.

Come, stack arms, men, pile on the rails,
    Stir up the camp-fire bright ;
No matter if the canteen fails,
    We'll make a roaring night !
Here, Shenandoah crawls along !
    There, burly Blue Ridge echoes strong,
To swell the Brigad's rousing song
    Of ' Stonewall Jackson's way.'

We see him now—the old slouch'd hat,
    Cock'd o'er his eye askew ;
The shrewd dry smile, the speech so pat,
    So calm, so blunt, so true ;

The 'Blue Light Elder' knows how well—
   Says he, 'That's Banks—he's fond of shell,
Lord save his soul!—we'll give him'—well
   That's 'Stonewall Jackson's way.'

Silence! ground arms! kneel all! caps off!
   Old 'Blue Light's' going to pray,—
Strangle the fool that dares to scoff!
   Attention, 'tis his way!
Appealing from his native sod,
   In *formâ pauperis* to God—
'Lay bare thine arm, stretch forth thy rod,'
   'Amen!' 'That's Stonewall's way.'

He's in the saddle now! Fall in!
   Steady! the whole brigade!
Hill's at the ford, cut off; we'll win
   His way out, ball and blade.
What matter if our shoes are worn?
   What matter if our feet are torn?
'Quick step! we're with him before dawn!'
   'That's Stonewall Jackson's way.'

The sun's bright lances rout the mists
   Of morning—and, by George!
Here's Longstreet, struggling in the list,
   Hemmed in an ugly gorge.
Pope and his Yankees, whipped before,
   'Bay'nets and grape!' hear Stonewall roar;
'Charge, Stuart! pay off Ashby's score'
   In 'Stonewall Jackson's way.'

Ah! maiden, wait, and watch, and yearn,
   For news of Stonewall's band,
Ah! widow, read with eyes that burn,
   That ring upon thy hand!
Ah! wife, sew on, pray on, hope on!
   Thy life shall not be all forlorn!
The foe had better ne'er been born
   That gets in 'Stonewall's way.'

JOHN MORGAN'S GRAVE.

Beneath the sward in old Virginia,
    Where the willow sheds its dew,
Near where stands the Nation's sentry
    Watching o'er our gallant few;
Near where strains of music rising,
    Thrill the hearts of comrades brave—
Near where Richmond's banners floating,
    Lies John Morgan in his grave.

Farewell, chieftain; you can never
    Throw your banner to the breeze again,
Your sword lies sheathed, while you, the wielder,
    Sleep the sleep that knows no pain.

Hollywood may boast of heroes,
    Yes, of a hero form who sleeps
Beneath the soil of a spot which ever
    The heroes of the South shall seek—
Shall seek to mourn a chieftain sleeping,
    Slain by treacherous hands we know:
But, oh ! his name, in fame reposing,
    Is honoured even by the foe.

His bugles a truce to him are sounding,
    A truce that heeds no battle-cry;
Victory oft had graced his banner,
    Nor feared he for his cause to die.
Quietly in his grave he's resting,
    Deaf to the cheers of the passing brave;
The lily and the wild-rose ever
    Will shed their nectar o'er his grave.

April 6, 1865.

THE GREATEST VICTORY OF THE WAR!

BY EUGENIE.

'La Bataille des Mouchoirs.'   Fought Friday, February 20, 1863.

Of all the battles, modern or old,
By poet sung or historian told ;
Of all the routs that ever were seen
From the days of Saladin to Marshal Turreene,
Or all the victories later yet won,
From Waterloo's field to that of Bull-run ;
All, all, must hide their fading light,
In the radiant glow of the handkerchief fight ;
And a pæan of joy must thrill the land,
When they hear of the deeds of Banks' band.

'Twas on the Levee, where the tide
    Of Father Mississippi flows ;
Our gallant lads, their country's pride,
    Won this great victory o'er her foes.
Four hundred rebels were to leave
    That morning for Secessia shades,
When down there came (you'd scarce believe)
    A troop of children, wives, and maids,
To wish farewells, to bid God-speed,
    To shed for them the parting tear,
To waft them kisses, as the meed
    Of praise to soldiers' hearts most dear.
They came in hundreds—thousands lined
    The streets, the roofs, the shipping too,
Their ribbons dancing in the wind,
    Their bright eyes flashing love's adieu.

'Twas then to danger we awoke,
    But nobly faced the unarmed throng,
And beat them back with hearty stroke,
    Till reinforcements came along.

We waited long—our aching sight
   Was strained in eager anxious gaze—
At last we saw the bayonets bright
   Flash in the sunlight's welcome blaze.
The cannon's dull and heavy roll
   Fell greeting on our gladdened ear,
Then fired each eye, then glowed each soul,
   For well we knew the strife was near.

Charge ! rang the cry, and on we dashed
   Upon our female foes,
As seas in stormy fury lashed
   Whene'er the tempest blows.
Like chaff their parasols went down,
   As on our gallants rushed ;
And many a bonnet, robe, and gown
   Was torn to shreds or crushed.
Though well we plied the bayonet,
   Still some our efforts braved,
Defiant both of blows and threat,
   Their handkerchiefs still waved.
Thick grew the fight, loud rolled the din,
   When—Charge ! rang out again,
And then the cannon thundered in,
   And scoured o'er the plain.
Down, 'neath th' unpitying iron heels
   Of horses, children sank,
While through the crowd the cannon wheels
   Mowed roads on either flank.
One startled shriek, one hollow groan,
   One headlong rush, and then—
Huzza ! the field was all our own,
   For we were Banks' men.

That night, released from all our toils,
   Our danger past and gone,
We gladly gathered up the spoils
   Our chivalry had won !

Five hundred kerchiefs we had snatched
　From rebel ladies' hands,
Ten parasols, two shoes (not matched),
　Some ribbons, belts, and bands,
And other things that I forgot;
　But then, you'll find them all
As trophies in that hallowed spot—
　The cradle—'Fanieul Hall.'

As long on Massachusetts' shore,
　Or on Green Mountain's side;
Or where Long Island's breakers roar,
　And by the Hudson's tide—
In times to come, when camps are lit,
　And fires brightly blaze,
While round the knees of heroes sit
　The young of happier days,
Who listen to their storied deeds,
　To them sublimely grand—
Then glory shall award its meed
　Of praise to Banks' band;
And Fame proclaim that they alone
　(In triumph's loudest note)
May wear henceforth, for valour shown,
　A woman's *petticoat* !

THE VIRGINIANS OF THE VALLEY.

BY DR. TICKNOR.

'Sic Jurat.'

The knightliest of the 'knightly race'
　Who, since the days of old,
Have kept the lamp of chivalry
　Alight in hearts of gold;

The kindliest of the kindly band
  Who rarely hated ease—
Who rode with Smith around the land,
  And Raleigh 'round the seas.

Who climbed the blue Virginia hills
  Amid embattled foes,
And planted there, in valleys fair,
  The Lily and the Rose,
Whose fragrance lives in many lands,
  Whose beauty stars the earth,
And lights the hearth of many a home
  With loveliness and worth!

We thought they slept! the sons who kept
  The names of noble sires,
And slumbered, while the dullness crept
  Around their vigil fires!
But still the Golden Horse-Shoe Knights
  Their Old Dominion keep,
Whose foes have found enchanted ground,
  But not a knight asleep!

Torch Hall, Georgia:
  December 1861.

RICHMOND ON THE JAMES.

A soldier boy from Bourbon lay gasping on the
  field,
When battle's shock was over, and the foe was forc'd
  to yield;
He fell, a youthful hero, before the foeman's aims,
On a blood-red field near Richmond, near Richmond
  on the James.

But one still stood beside him, his comrade in the
    fray—
They had been friends together through boyhood's
    happy day ;
And side by side had struggled, on fields of blood and
    flames,
To part that eve near Richmond, near Richmond on
    the James.

He said, 'I charge thee, comrade, the friend in days of
    yore,
Of the far, far distant dear ones that I shall see no
    more—
Tho' scarce my lips can whisper their dear and well-
    known names,
To bear to them my blessing from Richmond on the
    James.

'Bear my good sword to my brother, and the badge
    upon my breast
To the young and gentle sister that I used to love
    the best ;
But one lock from my forehead give the mother still
    that dreams
Of her soldier boy near Richmond, near Richmond
    on the James.

'Oh! I wish that mother's arms were folded round
    me now,
That her gentle hand could linger one moment on my
    brow,
But I know that she is praying where our blessed
    hearth-light gleams,
For her soldier's safe return from Richmond on the
    James.

'And on my heart, dear comrade, close lay those
    nut-brown braids
Of one that was the fairest of all our village maids ;

We were to have been wedded, but death the bride-
    groom claims,
And she is far, that loves me, from Richmond on the
    James.

' Oh, does the pale face haunt her, dear friend, that
    looks on thee ?
Or is she laughing, singing, in careless girlish glee ?
It may be she is joyous, and loves but joyous themes,
Nor dreams her love lies bleeding near Richmond on
    the James.

' And though I know, dear comrade, thou'lt miss me
    for awhile,
When their faces—all that lov'd thee—again on thee
    shall smile,
Again thou'lt be the foremost in all their youthful
    games,
But I shall lie near Richmond, near Richmond on
    the James.'

And far from all that loved him that youthful
    soldier sleeps,
Unknown among the thousands of those his country
    weeps ;
But no higher heart nor braver than his, at sunset's
    beams,
Was laid that eve near Richmond, near Richmond
    on the James.

The land is filled with mourning—from hall and cot
    left lone,
We miss the well-known faces that used to greet our
    own ;
And long, poor wives and mothers shall weep, and
    titled dames,
To hear the name of Richmond, of Richmond on the
    James.

BATTLE CALL.

BY ANNIE CHAMBERS KETCHUM.

Inscribed to her brave countrymen, the Cavaliers of the South.

Gentlemen of the South!
   Gird on your glittering swords!
Darkly along our borders fair
   Gather the northern hordes.
Ruthless and fierce they come
   At the fiery cannon's mouth,
To blast the glory of our land—
   Gentlemen of the South!

Ride forth in your stately pride,
   Each bearing on his shield
Ensigns your fathers won of yore
   On many a well-fought field.
Let this be your battle-cry,
   Even to the cannon's mouth:
Cor unum, via una! Onward!
   Gentlemen of the South!

Brave knights of a knightly race,
   Gordon and Stuart and Gray,
Show to the minions of the North
   How valour dares the fray!
Let them read on each stainless crest,
   At the belching cannon's mouth,
Decori decus addit avito—
   Gentlemen of the South!

Beauregard, Johnston, Lee!
   Douglas and Bradford and West!
Your gauntlets on many a bloody field
   Have stood the battle's test.

Animo, non astutia!
  March to the cannon's mouth,
Heirs of the brave dead centuries! Onward!
  Gentlemen of the South!

Call forth your stalwart men,
  Workers in brass and steel—
Bid the swart artisan come forth
  At sound of the trumpet's peal!
Give them your war-cry, Erskine!
  Fight! to the cannon's mouth!
Bid the men *Forward,* Douglas! *Forward!*
  Yeomanry of the South!

Brave hunters! ye have met
  The fierce black bear in the fray—
Ye have trailed the panther night by night,
  Ye have chased the fox by day!
Your prancing chargers pant
  To dash at the gray wolf's mouth—
Your arms are sure of their quarry! Onward!
  Gentlemen of the South!

Fight! that the lowly serf
  And the high-born lady still
May bide in their proud dependency,
  Free subjects of your will!
Teach the base North how ill,
  At the fiery cannon's mouth,
He fares who touches your household gods—
  Gentlemen of the South!

From mother, and wife, and child—
  From faithful and happy slave—
Prayers for your sakes ascend to Him
  Whose arm is strong to save.
                    D

We check the gathering tears,
  Though ye go to the cannon's mouth.
Dominus providebit! Onward!
  Gentlemen of the South!

Dunrobin Cottage, Memphis:
  May 1861.

MY WIFE AND CHILD.

Written by Gen. J. T. JACKSON, while an officer in Mexico.

The tattoo beats, the lights are gone,
  The camp around in slumber lies,
The night with solemn pace moves on,
  The shadow thickens o'er the skies;
But sleep my weary eyes has flown,
  And sad uneasy thoughts arise.

I think of thee, oh, dearest one,
  Whose love my early life hath blest—
Of thee and him, our baby son,
  Who slumbers on thy gentle breast!
God of the tender, frail, and lone,
  Oh! guard the gentle sleeper's rest!

And hover gently, hover near
  To her whose watchful eye is wet—
To mother, wife—the doubly dear,
  In whose young heart have freshly met
Two streams of love, so deep and clear,
  And cheer her drooping spirits yet.

Now, while she kneels before Thy throne,
  Oh, teach her, Ruler of the skies,
That while by Thy behest alone
  Earth's mightiest powers fall or rise,
No tear is wept to Thee unknown,
  No hair is lost, no sparrow dies;

That Thou canst stay the ruthless hands
  Of dark disease, and soothe its pain ;
That only by Thy stern commands
  The battle's lost, the soldier's slain ;
That from the distant sea or land,
  Thou bring'st the wanderer home again.

And when upon her pillow lone
  Her tear-wet cheek is sadly prest,
May happier visions beam upon
  The brightening current of her breast,
No frowning look nor angry tone
  Disturb the Sabbath of her rest.

Whatever fate those forms may show,
  Loved with a passion almost wild—
By day, by night, in joy or woe—
  By fears oppressed, or hopes beguiled,
From every danger, every foe,
  O God ! protect my wife and child !

'WHAT THO' THESE LIMBS.'

Written by Col. BEN ANDERSON, of Louisville, Kentucky, on the
  prison wall in Cincinnati, shortly before committing suicide.

What tho' these limbs be bound with iron cords,
Still am I free !
For Liberty can dwell amidst the clank of chains,
And in the gloom of dungeons,
As well as 'neath the leafy arches
Of the boundless forest.
Who can fetter the undying spirit,
Or circumscribe the limits of the mind ?
Far out beyond these prison walls
I roam adown the vistas
Of imagination—*and still am free* !

'LET THE DRUM'S DEEP TONES.'

By G. B. S., Cottage Home.

Let the drum's deep tones be muffled,
  Put the bugle far away,
Drape our battle-flag in mourning,
  For our hearts are sick to-day.
Yes, our hearts are sick with sorrow,
  Though the foeman's ranks we've riven,
Yet we cannot feel our victory—
  Not a shout of triumph's given.

And is it strange, oh, comrades,
  Is it strange that we should mourn?
Is it strange that on the night wind
  A low long wail is borne?
Oh! our leader, hast thou left us?
  Shall we never see thee more?
Wilt thou never lead the 'Old Brigade'
  To victory as of yore?

We shall miss the 'Stormy Petrel,'
  When the battle rages wild,
We shall miss his glowing orders,
  And his face so calm and mild.
We shall miss that kneeling figure,
  When the hour of strife draws near,
But the words that roused each patriot heart
  Will linger on each ear.

But his spirit will be with us
  In that dark and trying hour,
And we'll strike for 'Stonewall Jackson,'
  When the battle-cloud doth lower.
Yes, we'll dream that he is with us,
  And we'll conquer for his sake,
And we'll bear his banner onward,
  Till the tyrant's chains we break.

Oh ! our Jackson, thou hast left us,
   And a nation's loss thou art,
But we'll have thee ever near us,
   For thou'rt borne in every heart.
With the name of ' Stonewall Jackson '
   For our magic battle-cry,
With his glorious flag above us,
   We will conquer, or we'll die !

THE BATTLE BEFORE RICHMOND.

By G. B. S., 1862.

Slowly the great sun rose o'er Richmond's hills,
   Calmly the noble river waved along,
On every spray through which the zephyrs strayed
   A bird poured forth its gentle peaceful song ;
For ah ! they knew not ere the day be done,
A mighty battle should be fought and won !

Sweetly the morning blushed o'er Richmond's homes,
   But none save anxious hearts were throbbing there,
For from the depths of tender mothers' souls
   Went up for absent ones the earnest prayer.
Though anguish for the loved heaved in their breast,
To Him who gave those sons they looked for rest.

Those Southern mothers prayed, that summer morn,
   That when the battle-cloud should darkly lower,
Their sons and husbands in the fearful strife
   Might stand secure in that dark fatal hour—
Prayed that the Cause that called the loved away
Might beam as bright as that awakening day.

The sun rose o'er the snow-white tented field,
   It shone upon the many brave hearts there,
Each one a hero fit for poet's song,
   Each one well worthy a fond mother's prayer.
Firm resolution reigned in every eye,
Each one resolved to *conquer or to die.*

The drum calls loudly from the echoing hills,
   The patriot hosts are marshalling for the strife ;
No thought of fear comes o'er those Southern sons,
   They fight for homes, and those more dear than life—
They fight for freedom, and their native land,
To free themselves from the stern tyrant's hand.

Firmly each foot treads old Virginia's ground,
   Proudly the tri-barred banner floats in air ;
'Neath its protecting folds they know no fear,
   Each heart resolved to strive and conquer there.
The hours passed on— how changed that brilliant scene,
Naught looked as though a bright morn there had been !

Black clouds hung hovering o'er the scene below,
   The thunder of a thousand cannon woke the air,
Fiercely the sharp steel glittered through the veil
   That mantled o'er the dreadful conflict there ;
Fast flew the missiles, bearing death and woe,
And side by side in death slept friend and foe.

'The combat deepens.'—On, ye patriot hosts !
   Ye strive for Liberty upon this field !
Forward, ye heroes of Manassas' plain !
   For never can ye to the stern foe yield.
Forward, with cheers above the cannon's roar,
The Southrons rushed, and *Victory smiled once more* !

Onward ! for ever onward, Southrons brave !
   Think of your country, heroes tried and true !
Know that from yonder mountain's solemn heights
   A former revolution looks on you.
Nobly our Southron brothers fought that day,
Before their march the ruthless foe gave way.

Slowly that bright day faded into night,
   And o'er the scene black clouds hung heavily ;
While far above Virginia's mountain heights,
   Rolled, peal on peal, Heaven's grand artillery.
No stars shone forth upon that lonely night,
They dared not look upon so sad a sight.

And thou did'st veil thy shadowy form, O Moon!
  Thou could'st not look upon that field of death,
Where, even in the flush of victory,
  So many brave hearts drew the last long breath.
O Father! bless those dying patriots there,
Succor the South—this is our earnest prayer!

THE BATTLE OF MANASSAS.

Written by the Wife of Col. CLARK, 14th North Carolina
Regiment.

Dedicated to Gen. G. Y. BEAUREGARD, C. S. A.

Now glory to the Lord of Hosts!
  Oh, bless and praise His name,
That He hath battled in our cause,
  And brought our foes to shame!
And honor to our Beauregard,
  Who conquered in His might,
And for our children's children
  Won Manassas' bloody fight.
Oh, let our thoughtful prayers ascend,
  Our joyous praise resound,
For God, the God of victory,
  Our untried flag hath crowned!

They brought a mighty army,
  To crush us with a blow,
And in their pride they laughed to scorn
  The men they did not know.
Fair women came to triumph,
  With the heroes of the day,
When the 'boasting Southern Rebels'
  Should be scattered in dismay.
And for their conquering generals
  A lordly feast they spread;
But the wine in which we pledged them
  Was all of ruby red.

The feast was like Belshazzar's—
  In terror and dismay,
Before our conquering heroes,
  Their generals ran away.
God had weighed them in the balance,
  And His hand upon the wall,
At the taking of Fort Sumter,
  Had foredoomed them to their fall.
But they would not heed the warning,
  And scoffed in unbelief,
Till their scorn was changed to wailing,
  And their laughter into grief!

All day the fight was raging,
  And amid the cannon's peal,
Rang the cracking of our rifles,
  And the clashing of our steel;
But above the din of battle
  Our shout of triumph rose,
As we charged upon their batteries,
  And turned them on our foes.
We staid not for our fallen,
  And we thought not of our dead.
Until the day was ours,
  And the routed foe had fled!

But once our spirits faltered,
  Bee and Bartow both were down,
And our gallant Colonel Hampton,
  Lay wounded on the ground;
But Beauregard, God bless him!
  Led the legion in his stead,
And Johnston seized the colors,
  And waved them o'er his head.
E'en a coward must have followed,
  When such heroes led the way;
And no dastard blood was flowing
  In Southern veins that day!

But every arm was strengthened,
  And every heart was stirred,
When shouts of Davis ! Davis !
  Along our lines were heard.
As he rode into the battle,
  The joyful news flew fast ;
And the dying raised their voices,
  And cheered him as he passed.
Oh ! with such glorious leaders,
  In cabinet and field,
The gallant Southern chivalry
  Will die, but never yield !

But from the wings of victory
  The shafts of death were sped,
And our pride is dashed with sorrow
  When we count our noble dead ;
Though in our hearts they're living,
  And to our sons we'll tell
How gloriously our Fisher
  And our gallant Johnson fell;
And the name of each we'll cherish,
  As an honor to his State ;
And teach our boys to envy,
  And, if need be, meet their fate.

Then glory to the Lord of Hosts !
  Oh, bless and praise His name !
For He hath battled in our cause,
  And brought our foes to shame !
And honor to our Beauregard,
  Who conquered in His might,
And for our children's children
  Won Manassas' bloody fight !
Oh, let our grateful prayers ascend,
  Our joyous praise resound,
For God, the God of victory,
  Our untried flag hath crowned !

A MOTHER'S PRAYER.

'FAITH.'

Father, in the battle fray,
Shelter his dear head, I pray!
Nerve his young arm with the might
Of Justice, Liberty, and Right.
Where the red hail deadliest falls,
Where stern duty loudly calls,
Where the strife is fierce and wild—
Father! guard, oh, guard my child!

Where the foe rush swift and strong,
Madly striking for the wrong;
Where the clash of angry steel
Rings above the battle-field;
Where the stifling air is hot,
With bursting shell and whistling shot;
Father, to my boy's brave breast
Let no treacherous blade be pressed!

Father! if my woman's heart—
Frail and weak in every part—
Wanders from Thy mercy-seat,
After those dear roving feet,
Let Thy tender pitying grace
Every selfish thought erase!
If this mother-love be wrong,
Pardon, bless, and make me strong.

For when silent shades of night
Shut the bright world from my sight,
When, around the cheerful fire,
Gather brothers, sisters, sire:
Then I miss my boy's bright face
From the old familiar place,
And my sad heart wanders back
To tented field, and bivouac.

Often in my troubled sleep
Waking—wearily to weep—
Often dreaming he is near,
Calming every anxious fear—
Often startled by the flash
Of hostile swords that meet and clash,
Till the cannon's smoke and roar
Hide him from my sight no more.

Thus I dream, and hope, and pray,
All the weary hours away ;
But I know *his* cause is *just*,
And I centre all my trust
In Thy promise—'As thy day
So shall thy strength be'—alway !
Yet I need Thy guidance still ;
Father, let me do Thy will !

If new sorrow *should* befall,
If my noble boy should fall,
If the bright head I have blessed
On the cold earth find its rest ;
Still, with all the mother heart,
Torn, and quivering with the smart,
I *yield him*, 'neath Thy *chastening* rod,
To his *country* and his *God* !

ANNIE CARTER LEE,

Daughter of General Robert E. Lee ; died October 22, 1862, at
Jones' Springs, N. C.

'Earth to earth, and dust to dust'—
Saviour, in Thy word we trust ;
Sow we now our precious grain,
Thou shalt raise it up again ;
Plant we the terrestrial root
That shall bear celestial fruit ;

Lay a bud within the tomb,
That a flower in heaven may bloom :
Severed are no tender ties,
Tho' in earth's embrace she lies,
For the lengthening chain of love
Stretches to her home above.
Mother, in thy bitter grief,
Let this thought bring sweet relief;
Mother of an angel now,
God Himself hath crowned thy brow
With the thorns thy Saviour wore;
Blessed art thou evermore.
Unto Him thou didst resign
That precious life that erst was thine.

'Earth to earth—dust to dust '—
Sad the trial, sweet the trust;
Father, thou who see'st Death
Gathering grain at every breath,
As his sickle shaft he wields
O'er our bloody battle-fields :
Murmur not that now he weaves
This sweet flower into his sheaves ;
Taken in her early prime—
Gathered in her summer time—
Autumn's blast she shall not know,
Never shrink from Winter's snow.
Sharp the pang that thou must feel,
Sharper than the foeman's steel,
For thy fairest flower is hid
Underneath the coffin lid.
On her grave thou dropp'st no tear,
Warrior stern must thou appear,
Crushing back the bitter grief,
Which in vain demands relief.
Louder still thy country cries ;
At thy feet she bleeding lies,

And before the patriot now,
Husband, father, both must bow.
But, unnumbered are thy friends,
And from many a home ascends
Earnest heartfelt prayers for thee,
' As thy days, thy strength may be.'

THE SONG OF THE REBEL.

BY ESTEN COOK.

' Jackson's up!'—*Camp talk.*

Oh! not a heart in all our host
 But feels a noble thrill,
To see the bristling bayonets
 Of JACKSON on the hill ;
To know that he has scaled the RIDGE,
 And downward, onward pour
His legions to the field, from which
 The foe shall rise no more !

Make way for the ' Stormy Petrel,'
 Look how he rides the wind,
Down from the azure mountain—
 The calm days left behind ;
He comes on golden pinions
 Toward the glittering East,
And the eagle-brood are gathered
 To hold their bloody feast !

Hark ! how the long loud cheering
 Rings through the swaying pines,
And a thousand eyes are glowing
 Along the serried lines !
They know the great calm leader,
 In his old gray uniform—
And the brave hearts rush to meet him
 As they rush in the battle storm !

They know the man of KERNSTOWN—
　Of all that great campaign,
Far off in the snowy valley,
　Where he met with a grand disdain
The plundering Yankee cohorts,
　By SHIELDS and FREMONT led
To the field of PORT REPUBLIC—
　To sleep in a gory bed !

How he fell from the mountain passes
　Like a hawk upon his prey,
And the great host of M'CLELLAN
　Like a vapour passed away !
How charging at COLD HARBOR
　He swept them from his path,
As the dry leaves of the forest
　Are swept by the tempest's wrath.

So a health to STONEWALL JACKSON !
　That soul so brave and true,
That never a taint of craven guile
　Or shade of falsehood knew !—
Who never shrank from foeman's steel
　In the heart of the deadliest fight,
And bears on his radiant banner's fold—
　' May God defend the right ! '

In all the days of future years
　His name and fame shall shine—
The stubborn iron captain
　Of our old *Virginia Line* !
And men shall tell their children,
　Tho' all other memories fade,
That they fought with STONEWALL JACKSON
　In the old ' *Stonewall Brigade.* '

He comes !—his battle-flag aloft—
　His old brown coat more brown,
Than when the feeble arm of BANKS
　Essayed to strike him down ;

He comes with calm and simple air,
　　With kindly smile and eye—
The man for whom ten thousand braves
　　Would lay them down and die !

And if we cheer our hero,
　　Why not !　No glittering lord
Calls forth that shout : a soldier
　　Leaning upon his sword,
A way-worn Christian soldier,
　　Excites that grand acclaim,
To roll for ever through the walls
　　And down the halls of fame.

Beware, good General BURNSIDE,
　　The storm is roaring down !
The foaming crest is on the way,
　　And the skies begin to frown !
Beware, the Stormy Petrel
　　Is hovering o'er your camp—
And amid the tempest's howling
　　You may hear a steady 'tramp ! '

LONGSTREET is here to meet him—
　　That other warden strong,
Who watches at the temple gate,
　　To guard the shrine from wrong :
Large-minded, stout in action,
　　A fighter to the death—
No braver soul than LONGSTREET
　　E'er drew a human breath.

It blazed out at Manassas,
　　And in the hard-fought field
Of RICHMOND, where M'CLELLAN
　　Tried hard, but had to yield !
You know him by the steadfast eye,
　　And by the iron mouth—
A battle-charger, large and strong—
　　The 'War Horse ' of the South !

But hark ! a ringing bugle !—
  A merry clanking sound—
With the din of clattering hoof-strokes
  Upon the frosty ground !
And STUART with his sabre keen
  And floating plume appears,
Surrounded by his gallant band
  Of Southern cavaliers.

He rides his faithful ' Skylark,'
  With golden spurs on heel ;
Against the tall boot rattles
  His brand of burnished steel !
You read him by his lip and eye,
  His bearing, bold and free—
The Prince of Chieftains on a raid,
  And Pink of Chivalry !

The Yankee captains knew him—
  A sharp thorn in the side !
In the scouting of the VALLEY,
  And the wild Pamunkey ride—
In the dark midnight of Catlett's,
  And on MANASSAS' plain,
And when in Pennsylvania
  He charged their ranks amain.

And low at his side that phantom
  Erect on a snow-white steed !
With the pallid face and the fiery eyes,
  And the wounds that seem to bleed !
What august form has started
  Forth from his bloody shroud,
To ride at the head of the column
  When the wild charge clashes loud ?

The dead go fast ! the voices
  Of great men shout in the wind ;
Our hero has departed,
  But his brave soul stays behind.

Cold in the heart of ASHBY,
  That king of the battle-storm,
But it beats in the breast of STUART,
  And strikes with his heavy arm!

So a health to the daring leader,
  And all his merry men,
Who oft have hunted the Yankee wolf,
  And smoked him from his den;
Their deeds of chivalry bring back,
  The princely days of yore,
And the brave 'Earl Percy' lives again,
  With the very smile he wore!

Look! how the blue eyes brighten,
  The eager hand extends,
To greet his brother soldier—
  His faithful friend of friends!
See how two valiant spirits,
  Hot with the battle's breath,
Meet on the eve of conflict,
  Before the morn of death!

Long time ago they swore it—
  This friendship close and true;
They clasped brave hands, as says the song—
  'Ere this old coat was new;'
And in the hottest of the fight
  You'll see their forms appear—
The Chief of the Virginia Line,
  Beside the cavalier.

Around them are the noble band
  Of Paladins, who fight
In this our mighty struggle
  For God and for the Right.
The soldier face of PICKETT,
  The steady nerve of HILL,
The dashing LEES and HAMPTON
  Stout-hearted, strong of will.

E

BARKSDALE, that hardy fighter
  As ever mounted steed,
Brave GREGG, and COBB, and GARNETT,
  And JENKINS, good at need :
COOK, obstinate in combat,
  And KEMPER, hot of mood ;
And yonder, with the quiet smile,
  The honest face of HOOD !

Of HOOD, the hero-hearted,
  Who, in the darkest hour,
Stands like a lighthouse on a rock
  Whatever tempests lower :
Who wrote his name on GROVETON HEIGHTS
  And SHARPSBURG's bloody field,
A great and fearless soldier, trained
  In all—but how to yield.

Near there the younger captains
  In battle-trappings stand,
In red, and gold, and scarlet,
  A tried and trusty band.
Brave ROSSER, WICKHAM, MUNFORD,
  They come in long array ;
And BUTLER, GORDON, MARTIN,
  First in the raid or fray.

And still behind the Cavaliers
  Those other leaders come,
Who from the sullen cannon's mouth
  Hurl forth the bolt of doom ;
Cool WALKER, 'gallant PELHAM,'
  Of youthful modest mien—
And DEARING, with the smiling lips,
  The soul in battle keen.

No hardier band of gentlemen
  E'er drew the keen-edged brand,
Or rode amid the battle-smoke,
  To guard their native land !

For ever shall their famous deeds
  Shine on the glowing page—
Their name shall live through countless years—
  Our proudest heritage!

One form alone remains behind,
  And, lo! the figure comes,
Not with the tinsel Yankee pomp,
  Or din of rolling drums—
Wrapped in his old gray riding-cape—
  A grizzled chevalier,
See LEE, our spotless Southern Knight,
  'Without reproach or fear!'

We know him well, our captain,
  The foremost man of all,
Whom, tho' the red Destruction lower,
  No peril can appal!
We know how he struck M'CLELLAN
  In his trebly guarded lines,
And BULLY POPE sent flying
  Through the dim Manassas pines!

All honour to the Chieftain
  With the calm undaunted mien,
The honest old Virginia blood,
  And the great broad soul serene!
Though all the hounds of Ruin howl,
  These rations shall be free,
For the Red-Cross flag is borne aloft
  By the stalwart hand of LEE!

The Chieftain of our Chieftains,
  Virginia claims her son—
But for the whole great Southern race
  His deeds have glory won.
For the blood of 'LIGHT HORSE HARRY'
  Burns in a larger soul,
As true to the call of honour
  As the needle to the pole!

As true! and who but loves him,
  The man to us so dear!
Whom soil of base detraction
  Has never dared come near!
Who keeps his lordly path unmoved
  Through calm or storm—and hears
Even now the calm Historic Voice
  From out the future years!

Such is our band of heroes,
  Who fight the bitter fight
Here on our sacred Southern soil
  For our ancient English right!
Who meet and greet brave JACKSON
  Upon his rapid way,
For whom all patriotic hearts
  Unceasing praise and pray!

So a health to STONEWALL JACKSON,
  To LONGSTREET brave as steel;
To STUART, with the fearless soul,
  A knight from plume to heel!
And last to LEE our General,
  Beneath whose flag we go,
To test the edge of Southern steel
  On a vulgar brutal foe.

Camp 'No Camp:'
  December 1, 1862.

THE SOUTHRONS O!

By the cross upon our banner,
  Glory of our Southern sky,
Swear we now, a band of brothers
  Free to live and free to die;
We have sworn—as freemen never
  Swear, who live to break their vow:
Northron, by the *right* denied us,
  Ye shall never rule us now!

By our brave ones lost in battle,
  Best and gentlest of our land,
Fighting with your Northern hirelings,
  Face to face, and hand to hand ;
By a sacrifice so priceless,
  By the spirits of the slain,
Swear we now, our Southern heroes
  Shall not thus have died in vain.

Wide and deep the breach between us,
  Rent by *hatred's* poisoned darts,
And ye cannot now cement it
  With the blood of Southern hearts.
Streams of gore that gulf shall widen,
  Running strong, and deep, and red,
Severing you from us *for ever*,
  While there is a drop to shed.

Think you we will brook the insults
  Of your fierce and ruffian chief
Heaped upon our dark-eyed daughters,
  Stricken down and pale with grief ?
Think you, while astounded nations
  Curse your malice, we will bear
Foulest wrongs, with God to call on,
  Arms to do, and hearts to dare ?

When we prayed in peace to leave you,
  Answering came a battle-cry !
Then we *swore that oath* which freemen
  Never swear who fear to die !
Northron, come ! and ye shall find us
  Heart to heart, and hand to hand,
Shouting to the God of battle—
  Freedom and our *native land* !

NO ONE WRITES TO ME.

The list is called, and one by one
    The anxious crowd now melts away;
I linger still, and wonder why
    No letter comes for me to-day
Are all my friends in Dixie dead?
    Or would they all forgotten be?
What have I done, what have I said,
    That no one writes a line to me?
        It's mighty queer!

I watch the mails each weary day,
    With anxious eyes the list o'errun,
I envy him whose name is called,
    But love him more who gets not one.
For I can sympathise with him,
    And feel how keen his grief must be,
Since I'm an exile from my home,
    And no one writes a line to me,
        I do declare!

Within a quiet happy home,
    Far, far in Dixie's sunny clime,
There dwells a quiet happy maid,
    Who wrote to me in bygone time;
Now, others from their loved ones hear,
    In tender letters, loving, free,
Yet here I've been this half a year,
    And no one writes a line to me—
        We're not estranged!

Will no one write me just a line,
    To say that I'm remembered yet?
You cannot guess how much delight
    I'd feel, could I a letter get—

Could I but hear from some kind friend,
  Whose face I ne'er again may see :
Will some one now my anguish end ?
  If some one doesn't write to me,
     I'll—get exchanged !

Johnson's Island :
  January 1, 1864.

THE CONQUERED BANNER.

BY MOINA.

Furl that banner for 'tis *weary*,
Round its staff 'tis drooping dreary,
  Furl it, fold it, it is best ;
For there's not a man to wave it,
And there's not a sword to save it,
And there's not one left to lave it
In the blood which heroes gave it ;
And its foes now scorn and brave it—
  Furl it, *hide* it, let it rest.

Take that banner down, 'tis tattered !
Broken is its staff and shattered,
And the valiant hosts are scattered,
  Over whom it floated high.
Oh ! 'tis hard for us to fold it—
Hard to think there's none to hold it—
Hard that those who once unrolled it,
  Now must furl it with a sigh.

Furl that banner, furl it sadly,
Once, ten thousands hailed it gladly,
And ten thousands wildly, madly,
  Swore it should for ever wave :
Swore that foeman's sword could never
Hearts like theirs entwined dissever,
Till that flag should float for ever
  O'er their freedom or their grave.

Furl it ! for the hands that grasped it,
And the hearts that fondly clasped it,
   Cold and dead are lying low ;
And that banner, it is trailing,
While around it sounds the wailing
   Of its people in their woe.

For, though conquered, they adore it,
Love the cold dead hands that bore it,
Weep for those who fell before it,
Pardon those who trailed and tore it;
But, oh ! wildly they deplore it
   Now, who furl and fold it so !

Furl that banner—true, 'tis gory,
Yet 'tis wreathed around with glory,
And 'twill live in song and story,
   Though its folds are in the dust ;
For its fame on brightest pages,
Penned by poets and by sages,
Shall go sounding down the ages—
   Furl its folds though now we must.

Furl that banner, softly, slowly,
Treat it gently, it is holy—
   For it droops above the dead ;
Touch it not, unfold it never,
Let it droop there, *furled* for ever,
   For its people's *hopes* are dead.

WHEN PLEASURE'S FLOWERY PATHS.

By a Prisoner in solitary confinement.

When pleasure's flowery paths I trod,
   My eyes were bent on earth alone,
I lifted not my soul to God—
   Nor praised the glories of His throne.

Earth was so full of transient bliss,
   It occupied my thankless heart ;
I asked no other world than this,
   And now a Dungeon is my part.

Here, no responsive glance can tell
   The yearnings of a loving soul,
Confined alone within my cell,
   The waves of Anguish o'er me roll.

Look up, faint heart ! a Saviour stands,
   His meek eyes in forgiveness bent
To where you stand with outstretched hands,
   And calls you, sinner, to repent.

Ah, yes ! my God ! I did go wrong,
   Ere woe and troubles o'er me came;
'Tis good that sorrows on me throng,
   I learn Thy statutes, praise Thy name.

Then help me, Lord ! stand by my side,
   My stricken breast Thy hand will bind;
Give me, whatever ills betide,
   A patient heart, a soul resigned.

And if from this you lift me up,
   Let not prosperity betray ;
But let me take Thy *Bread* and *Cup*,
   And grateful, praise Thy name alway.

May 28, 1865.

REDEEMED !

By a Prisoner in solitary confinement.

What, though the wrong I have defied,
   And smote it with the fleshy sword ;
Like Peter, I have thrice denied
   My Master, and my gracious Lord.

Seventy times seven I've been forgiven,
   When I have sinned against my God;
Still has His Holy Spirit striven
   To save me from the avenging rod.

Ten thousand talents did I owe—
   My Lord, forgive the heavy debt;
Unto my brother shall I show
   Less mercy, and my Lord's forget?

No, Lord! let me to others give
   The pardon Thou hast shown to me;
Patient and thankful let me live,
   Redeemed from death, from sin set free.

May 31, 1865.

I SHALL NOT DIE.

By a Prisoner in solitary confinement at Fort Delaware.

I felt the pride of intellect,
   I had the power of conscious strength;
I knew no flaw, saw no defect
   In all my nature's breadth and length.

My purposes I knew were good,
   My moral bases seemed secure;
And pride, like some tall phantom, stood
   And told me that my heart was pure.

How often have I given proof
   How weak and poor was their defence;
For, when we think we stand aloof
   From weakness—then our sins commence.

How often have I put to test
   The mercy of my Judge on high,
Pity, not justice, gives me rest,
   And Jesus says, I shall not die.

On Jesus' words I build my hope,
   On Jesus' aid I now rely ;
His spirit with the foe will cope,
   His promise is—I shall not die.

THE BATTLE OF ST. PAUL'S.

Fought in New Orleans, October 12, 1862.

SUNG BY A LOUISIANA SOLDIER.

Come, boys, and listen, while I sing
   The greatest fight yet fought—
That time the hated Yankee
   A real Tartar caught.
'Twas not the first Manassas,
   Won by our Beauregard,
Nor Perryville, nor Belmont,
   Though Polk then hit him hard ;
Nor was it famous Shiloh,
   Where Sydney Johnston fell—
No ! these were mighty battles,
   But a greater I will tell.
'Twas fought on Sunday morning,
   Within the Church's walls,
And shall be known in hist'ry
   As the battle of St. Paul's.
The Yankee, Strong, commanded
   For Butler, the abhorr'd—
And the Reverend Mr. Goodrich
   Bore the banner of the Lord.
The bell had ceased its tolling,
   The service nearly done,
The Psalms and Lessons over,
   The Lord's Prayer just begun ;
When, as the priest and people
   Said, 'Hallowed be Thy name,
A voice in tones of thunder
   His order did proclaim :

' As this house has been devoted
   To great Jehovah's praise,
And no prayer for Abra'm Lincoln
   Within its walls you raise,
Therefore, of rank Secession
   It is an impious nest,
And I stop all further service,
   And the clergyman arrest ;
And, in name of General Butler,
   I order furthermore,
That this assembly scatter,
   And the sexton close the door.'
Up rose the congregation—
   We men were all away,
And our wives and little children
   Alone remained to pray.
But when have Southern women
   Before a Yankee quailed ?
And these, with tongues undaunted,
   That Lincolnite assailed.
In vain he called his soldiers—
   Their darts around him flew,
And the ' *Strong* ' man then discovered
   What a woman's tongue can do.
Some cried, ' We knew that Butler
   On babes and women warr'd,
But we did not think to find him
   In the temple of the Lord.'
Some pressed around their pastor,
   Some on the villain gazed,
Who, against the Lord's anointed,
   His dastard arm had raised.
Some said, ' E'en to a Yankee
   We would not do such wrong
As to mistake another
   For the gallant Major Strong ;
So we'll look upon the hero
   Till his face we cannot doubt,'—

While a stout old lady shouted,
  '*Do some one kick him out.*'
'Don't touch him,' cried another,
  'He is worthy of his ruler,
For he fights with women braver
  Than he fought at Ponchatoula.'
But when the storm raged fiercest,
  And hearts were all aflame,
Like oil on troubled waters,
  The voice of blessing came.
For. though with angry gestures
  The Yankee bid him cease,
The priest, with hands uplifted,
  Bid his people go in peace ;
And called down heavenly blessings
  Upon that tossing crowd,
While the men their teeth were clenching,
  And the women sobbing loud.
And then, with mien undaunted,
  He passed along the aisle,
The gallant Yankee hero
  Behind him all the while.
'You'd better bring a gunboat,
  For that's your winning card,
Said a haughty little beauty,
  As the '*Strong*' man called a guard
'Tis only 'neath their shelter
  You Yankees ever fight,'
Cried another spunky woman
  Who stood upon his right.
But the Major thought a cannon
  (If his men could not succeed
In clearing off the sidewalk)
  Would be all that he should need.
And I guess his light artill'ry
  'Gainst Christ Church he will range,
When his ' base of operations '
  Next Sunday he shall ' change.'

'Twas thus the tyrant Butler,
  'Mid women's sobs and tears,
Seized a priest before the altar
  He had served for twenty years.
We know in darkest ages
  A Church was holy ground,
Where from the hand of justice
  A refuge might be found;
And from the meanest soldier
  To the highest in the land,
None dared to touch the fugitive
  Who should within it stand.
'Twas left the beastly Butler
  To violate its walls,
And to be known in future
  As the Victor of St. Paul's.
He has called our wives 'She-adders,'
  And he shall feel their sting,
For the voice of outraged woman
  Through every land shall ring.
He shall stand with Austrian Haynau
  Upon the rolls of fame,
And bear to latest ages
  A base dishonoured name.

THERE IS NO PEACE.

BY G. B. S.

They tell us that glad peace once more has smiled
  Upon this land from out the summer sky;
They tell us that war's voice is hushed and stilled,
  They whisper—'Let the Past forgotten lie.'

Away, away! there's mockery in the sound,
  There is no music in that glad word *Peace*;
Forget! breathe not that word again—*forget*!
  As well command the heart's wild throb to cease.

Can there be peace while e'en one foeman's tread
    Pollutes the soil of our Southern land?
Can there be peace while one sweet Southern home
    Lies all in ruins 'neath the foeman's hand?

Can we forget—when all the summer air
    Is filled with dirges for the fallen braves?
Can we forget—when loved ones come no more,
    And hope's bright blossoms fade on new-made
        graves?

Each Southern heart is lone and sad to-day,
    We miss the forms that never come again;
But, oh! a martyr's halo crowns each brow,
    And martyrs never, *never* die in vain.

O'erwhelmed but *all unconquered* is our land;
    Home of the brave! proud hearts still cling to thee!
O'erwhelmed *but for a time*, we wait, we wait:
    God has decreed *the South shall yet be free*!

We look to Him—He in His own good time'
    Will sweep away the clouds 'neath which we dwell;
With trusting hearts we wait that chosen hour:
    Sons of the noble South! *all will be well.*

Cottage Home, 1865.

EXCHANGED.

From his drear prison, by Erie's bleak shore,
    He is borne to his last resting-place,
The glance of affection and friendship no more
    Shall rest on the captive's worn face;
The terms of his cartel his God has arranged,
And the victim of prison has at last been 'ex-
    changed.'

His comrades consign his remains to the grave
  With a tear and a sigh of regret;
He died far away from the land of the brave,
  From the land he could never forget;
'Mid the scenes of his childhood his fancy last ranged,
Ere the sorrows of life and its cares were 'ex-
    changed.'

The clods of the island now rest on the head
  That the havoc of battle had spared,
On the field that was strewn with the dying and
    dead,
  Whose perils and dangers he shared.
From home and from all that he loved long estranged,
Death pitied the captive, and had him 'exchanged.'

Johnson's Island.

THE DEATH OF POLK.

We hear a solemn saddening sound,
    A mournful knell;
From every sacred spire tolls forth
    The funeral bell.
Through all the land a wail goes out:
    The nation weeps—
And voices full of tears proclaim
    A hero sleeps.
For ever stilled, the noble heart
    Within his breast,
The patriot, soldier, martyr, priest,
    Is now at rest.
Then everywhere let joy be hushed,
    And bow each head;
Truth, Chivalry and Freedom weep—
    For Polk is dead.

And near the spot where fell our chief,
    We wait the foe;
But we weep not, though all our hearts
    Are filled with woe.
Our sobs are hushed where cannons roar,
    And triggers fall;
The tears we shed are grape and shell,
    And Minnié ball.
A thought in dying sternly throbs
    Our hearts among;
And vengeance speaks in every eye,
    On every tongue.
For this, O God, we watch and wait
    From hour to hour;
Be ours, Almighty One, the arms,
    And Thine the power.

THE ANGEL OF THE CHURCH.

BY W. G. S.

The enemy, from his camp on Morris Island, has, in frequent letters in the Northern papers, avowed the object at which they aim their shells in Charlestown to be the spire of St. Michael's Church.* Their practice shows that these avowals are true. Thus far they have not succeeded in their aim. 'Angels of the churches' is a phrase applied by St. John, with reference to the seven churches of Asia. The Hebrews recognised an 'angel of the church,' in their language 'Shellack Zibbor,' whose office may be described as that of a watchman or guardian of the church. Daniel says (iv. 13), 'Behold a watcher and a holy one come down from heaven.' The practice of naming churches after tutelary saints originated, no doubt, in the conviction that when the church was pure, and the faith true, and the congregation pious, these guardian angels, so chosen, would accept the office assigned them. They were generally chosen from the cherubim and seraphim; those who, according to St. Paul (Col. i. 16), represented thrones, dominions, principalities, and powers. According to the Hebrew traditions, St. Michael was

* St. Michael's Church was opened for divine worship, Feb. 1, 1761.

the head of the first order, Gabriel of the second, Uriel of the third, and Raphael of the fourth. St. Michael is the warrior angel, who led the hosts of the sky against the powers of the princes of the air; who overthrew the dragon, and trampled him under foot. The destruction of the Anaconda, in his hands, would be a similar undertaking.

Assuming for our people a hope not less rational than that of the people of Nineveh, we may reasonably build upon the guardianship and protection of God, through His angels, 'a great city of sixty thousand souls,' which has been for so long a season the subject of His care.

These notes will supply the adequate illustrations for the Ode which follows.

Ay, strike with sacrilegious aim
  The Temple of the Living God,
Flint, iron bolt, and seething flame,
  Through aisles which holiest feet have trod.
Tear up the altar, spoil the tomb,
  And, raging with demoniac ire,
Send down in sudden crash of doom
  That grand old sky-sustaining spire.

That spire for full a hundred years
  Hath been a people's point of light;
That shrine hath warmed their souls to tears,
  With strains well worthy Salem's height;
That sweet clear music of its bells,
  Made liquid-soft in Southern air,
Still thro' the heart of memory swells,
  And wakes the hopeful soul to prayer.

Along the shores for many a mile,
  Long ere they owned one beacon mark,
It caught and kept the Day-God's smile,
  The guide for every wandering bark;*
Averting from our homes the scaith
  Of fiery bolt in storm-cloud driven,
The Pharos to the wandering Faith,
  It pointed every prayer to Heaven!

* The height of this steeple makes it the principal landmark for the pilots.—*Dalcho's History*, 1819.

Well may ye, felons of the time,
　Still loathing all that's pure and free,
Add this to many a hateful crime
　'Gainst Peace and sweet Humanity.
Ye, who have wrapt our towns in flame,
　Defiled our shrines, befoul'd our homes,
But fitly turn your murderous aim
　Against Jehovah's ancient domes.

Yet, though the grand old Temple falls,
　And downward sinks the lofty spire,
Our faith is stronger than our walls,
　And soars above the storm and fire.
Ye shake no faith in souls made free
　To tread the paths their fathers trod,
To fight and die for Liberty,
　Believing in the avenging God !

Think not—though long His anger stays—
　His justice sleeps, His wrath is spent :
The arm of vengeance but delays
　To make more dread the punishment !
Each impious hand that lights the torch
　Shall wither ere the bolt shall fail,
And the bright Angel of the Church,
　With seraph shield, avert the ball.

For still we deem, as taught of old,
　That where the Faith the altar builds,
God sends an Angel from His fold
　Whose sleepless watch the Temple shields ;
And to His flock with sweet accord,
　Yields their fond choice from thrones and powers ;
Thus Michael, with his fiery sword
　And golden shield, still champions ours !

And he who smote the Dragon down,
　And chain'd him thousand years of time,
Need never fear the Boa's frown,
　Though loathsome in his spite and slime.

He, from the topmost heights surveys,
   And guards the shrines our fathers gave,
And we, who sleep beneath His gaze,
   May well believe His power to save!

Yet, if it be that for our sin
   Our Angel's term of watch is o'er,
With proper prayer, true faith must win
   The guardian watcher back once more!
Faith, brethren of the Church, and prayer—
   In blood and sackcloth, if it need—
And still our spire shall rise in air—
   Our temple—though our people bleed!

January 1864.

THE BONNIE DUNDEE OF THE BORDER.

BY CLARINE RIRNARDE.

(Inscribed to Col. Wm. S. Hawkins, of the Western Army.)

Oh, lightly his proud plume floats over the field,
   And the battle-god smileth his honors above him,
All bright is the blade our young hero doth wield,
   And many the fond and true spirits that love him;
So proudly he charges the cohorts of blue,
   And breaks every line in the wildest disorder—
Who fears when he's leading, so gallant and true,
   The Bonnie Dundee of the Border!

All blue is his eye, and all dark is his hair,
   And his voice like a silvery bugle, when calling
His men to the charge, there to do and to dare,
   Tho' death-shots around them so thickly are falling.
In the council and camp, or where blood runs like
     rain,
   He's ever the foremost for law and for order,
His flag without spot, and his shield without stain—
   The Bonnie Dundee of the Border!

From the cottage and hall he has gathered his men,
  And they rally for fight 'neath the leaf-shadowed
    wild wood,
And their gallop is heard by the height and the glen,
  As they rush to defend the dear homes of their
    childhood.
And first in the fray their gay chieftain shall be,
  He needs naught of praise from the servile ap-
    plauder,
He'll gain his reward when his country is free—
  The Bonnie Dundee of the Border !

In the white days of peace when they honour the
    bold,
  With garlands of triumph and wild ringing pœan,
By many a hearthside the tale shall be told
  Of the deeds and the fame of our young Tennessean.
When the flash of his sword, and his rifle's keen ring,
  Oft startled the foe and dismayed the marauder ;
And praises and blessings around him shall cling—
  The Bonnie Dundee of the Border !

THE HERO WITHOUT A NAME.

BY COL. W. S. HAWKINS, C. S. A.

I loved, when a child, to seek the page
  Where war's proud tales are grandly told ;
And to dream of the might of former age,
  In the brave good days of old.
When men, for virtue and honor fought
  In serried pride, 'neath their banners bright
By the fairy hands of beauty wrought,
  And 'broidered with ' God and Right.'

And there I read of Sir Launcelot true,
  Whose deeds have been sung in a nobler strain ;
And of Roderick the Bold, who his falchion drew
  In the cause of his native Spain.

In thought I beheld gay Sidney ride,
 His white plume dotting the field's expanse;
And Bayard, who came like the rush of the tide,
 As he struck for the lilies of France.

On the crags of Scotland, there I saw
 With the hair of golden hue—Montrose;
And swarthy Douglas, whose name was awe,
 In the homes of his English foes.
There was Winkelried, in the Swiss land famed,
 And the mountaineer's boast, devoted Tell,
Who smiled as before his shaft, well aimed,
 His country's tyrant fell.

'Neath Erin's flag with its glad 'Sunburst'
 Was Emmet, who stands in that martyr-van,
Whose blood sanctified the gibbet accursed,
 Where he died for the rights of man.
There was Light-horse Harry, the first in the fray,
 There was Marion leading his cavaliers,
And Washington, too, whose grave to-day
 Is the shrine of the patriot's tears.

Those splendid forms were a part of the throng
 That delighted me, moving in pageants grand
Through the wastes of time, and the fields of song,
 From the legends of every land.
But I little hoped myself to see
 A spirit akin to those stately men,
Nor thought that great hearts like theirs could be
 In a prison's crowded pen.

Yet I've seen in the wards of the hospital there
 A hero, I fancy, as peerless of soul,
A pale-faced boy whose home is fair,
 Where the waters of Cumberland roll.

On his narrow cot, in that narrow room,
   Where the music he hears is the sigh and the
      groan,
He lies through the day's long pain and gloom—
   But he never makes a moan.

They hewed him down with their blades of steel,
   When the troopers charged from the camps of the
      foe—
But he was not killed, although I feel
   It would have been better so ;
For my heart within me is very sad,
   As I sit and hold his wasted hand,
And hear him tell of the times that were glad,
   In our dear and sunny land.

There are hours, again, in his fever's heat,
   When his restless fancies fly to his home,
When he talks of the scythes in the falling wheat,
   And of reapers that go and come ;
Of his boyish mates, in their frolicsome glee,
   Thro' the cedarn glades and the woodlands dim,
And how he carved there, on many a tree,
   A name that was dear to him ;

Of the sweet wild roses that scatter the lights
   Through the cottage door and the window-panes,
And October's haze on the far-off heights,
   And the quiet country lanes ;
Of the rivulet's plash, and the song of birds,
   And the corn-rows standing like men with spears ;
Of his mother's prayers, and her loving words,
   And her cheeks all wet with tears.

And I seem to see her as the autumn leaves
   Are silently falling in the glen—
As the swallows come back to the sheltering eaves,
   Where he shall not come again.

Then I rejoice that she cannot see
  How the blight has stained her fairest bloom;
I am glad that her steps will never be
  Beside his Northern tomb.

And I think of another who watches too,
  When the early stars are bright on the hill,
Nor knows that his heart, so confiding and true,
  Will soon be for ever still.
Ah! many in vain to their hopes shall cling,
  Thro' the dreary morn and the mournful eve,
And memory alone shall its solace bring
  To a thousand hearts that grieve.

My comrade will last but a little while,
  For I see on every succeeding day
A fainter flush, but a sweeter smile,
  Over his features play.
He knows that until he is under the sod,
  These walls—little better—shall shut him in;
But his soul puts trust in the Lamb of God,
  Who taketh away all sin.

And somehow I think when our lives are done,
  That this humble hero without a name
Will be greater up there than many a one
  Of the high-born men of fame.
And I know I would rather have to-day
  The crown he will wear, with its fadeless bloom,
Than Roderick's helm so golden and gay,
  Or Sidney's snow-white plume.

O prisoner boy! that I were as near
  As you are now to that 'Shining Shore,'
Where the waters of life and of love are clear,
  And weeping shall be no more.

It cannot be thus—yet in God's own time
  He will call His weary ones home to rest,
And the beautiful angels, with song and with chime,
  Shall welcome each mortal guest.

Camp Chase:
  October 1864.

DEAD!

By Col. W. S. Hawkins, C. S. A. (Prisoner of War).

Dead! with no loving hand to part
  The soft hair back from his pallid brow—
Dead! and there is no mourning heart
  To follow the captive now.

Gone! from the Prison, lone and drear,
  With his patient smile and his gentle ways—
Gone! where the jasper walls appear,
  And the Beautiful Gates of Praise.
Roses! that bloom by his home in glee,
  Whose distant odors are sweetly shed,
Let the dew in each delicate chalice be
  As tribute-tears to the dead.
And song-birds! trill to the throbbing eve,
  When the shadows are gathering dusk and dim,
A music to soothe our souls that grieve,
  And a low soft dirge to him.

Comrades! who slept beside him there,
  Where the mountain torrents brawl and roar,
Will your dreams to-night by the camp-fire's glare
  Tell that he comes no more?
Ah! the morning will shine with the glory-crown,
  And the cheery and dimpling air for his breath,
And you will not know that his sun's gone down
  In the evening skies of death.

Mother! make room 'mid your memories dear,
   For one that is sadder and sweeter yet,
There's a newborn joy for thee up there,
   Where the soul knows no regret.
The leaves of the autumn fall apace,
   The better to feed the blossoms of spring;
So, from thy life is shed some grace,
   A holier grace to bring.

Sister! 'twould wring your soul to know,
   That the cheeks you have kissed are so pale and
      thin;
And the fire's gone out from the eyes' deep glow,
   Where such loving glance hath been.
But the eyes that seemed so glazed and dim,
   Are bright enough in the courts above,
Where the golden harps of the seraphim
   Chime to the touch of Love.

Maiden! upon whose heart to-night
   His tokens of faith are proudly prest,
He waits for thee 'mid the Isles of Light,
   In the mansions of the blest.
When the summoning angel in splendour came,
   And life's star sank in a swift eclipse,
He murmured of you, and your tender name
   Seems yet on his silent lips.

Sepulchre! thou shalt be holy ground,
   Since to thee such peerless charge is given,
Oh! guard it well, till the heralds sound
   The bugle-call of Heaven.
And Freedom! tho' he fell not on thy field,
   He still has died for thee and for thine;
Make his record, then, on thy proudest shield,
   Where the names of thy truest shine!

Camp Chase, Ohio:
   March 1865.

THE VICTORY OF FAITH.

By Col. W. S. HAWKINS, C. S. A. (Prisoner of War).

At the trumpet's blast, the gates flew wide,
    And thousands packed the Court,
Before the Roman lords that day,
    The Captives furnished sport.
The Sun's broad orb went up the sky,
    And tipped the scene with gold,
And far beyond the Claudian way
    The yellow Tiber rolled.

The Gladiators, first in strife,
    Their glittering weapons crossed,
And furious then in mortal surge
    The waves of conflict tossed.
Strong men were there, whose children played
    By Danube's sluggish tide;
And those whose homes lay, sweet and fair,
    Along the Taurus' side.

Those fierce-eyed tigers of the Lybian wild,
    Leaped forth into the Cirque,
And spotted leopards, lithe and strong,
    Began their horrid work.
And howls of pain, and yells of wrath,
    Filled all the trembling air,
While Roman knights applauded loud,
    And smiled the Roman fair.

At length the heralds far, proclaimed,
    The last best scene of all,
And led a Christian martyr forth,
    In the fetters' grievous thrall ;
No youth with form of manly strength—
    No feeble gray-haired sire—
A soft-eyed maiden, sweet and pure,
    To whet a lion's ire.

She stood—her timid glance cast down,
 And trembling like a fawn,
Which baying hounds and hunters rude
 Surround at hour of dawn;
One white hand slowly lifted up
 The cruel galling chain,
And one pressed close her beating heart,
 For there were grief and pain.

She thought of home and peaceful joys—
 Her father, strong and proud,
Her mother's clinging faithful soul
 By weight of misery bowed.
Her sisters and her brothers fond—
 And one she could not speak,
But at the slightest thought of *him*
 A blush suffused her cheek.

And as they neared the monster's den,
 With triple iron bound,
Through all the spectacles, his might
 With bloodiest triumphs crowned.
White his large teeth, and dark and red
 His yawning dreadful throat,
His eyes with gore a-fire, and seemed
 On this new prize to gloat.

He rose and shook his bristling mane,
 And clamoured at his door,
The far-off hill-tops echoed loud
 His deep resounding roar.
So in the Nubian waste he looked,
 When roused by foe for fight,
And such a glance and such a roar
 Filled every soul with fright.

They loosed her chain and left her there,
 In all her maiden's grace,
And only starlike Faith lit up
 The heaven of her face.

THE VICTORY OF FAITH.

The rusted hinges turned, and forth
  The brute in fury sprung,
His lips all flecked with wrathful foam,
  And swelled his lolling tongue.

The breathless thousands rose to see
  That youthful martyr die,
But, ah ! what magic spell is that
  Whose lustre fills her eye ?
Her sweet lips part—her full heart throbs—
  Her beauteous hands are raised ;
The cruel beast forgets his wrath,
  Before that look amazed.

She kneels, and on the yielding sand
  Her rounded form sinks low,
Down in her soul the maiden prays
  Unto her God—and so
The pure appeal is borne on high
  By watching angels fleet,
And now the humble lion comes,
  And crouches at her feet.

Her little hand is softly laid
  Upon his tawny mane,
Her tender eyes are wet with tears,
  Like violets after rain.
The watching courtiers shake the ring
  With thunderous acclaim,
But her weak lips can only shape
  Her heavenly Father's name.

The Emperor rose in purpled state,
  And bade his minions bear
The ransomed maiden forth again
  To freedom's thrilling air.
And stately Priests, their rites ordained
  Within the templed grove,
Ascribing praise to Juno fair,
  And to Olympian Jove.

But heathen gods are wood and stone——
    Hers was a Father dear,
To whom in childish trust and love
    Her fainting heart drew near.
When lions rude, of doubt and sin,
    Their brutal force prepare,
Before a frowning world our help,
    Like hers, will be in prayer.

And let the Church in these dark days
    Stand bravely at her post,
Tho' cruel wars and strifes abound,
    And Satan leads his hosts:
They gnash their lion fangs at her,
    But, oh! they gnash in vain,
For God will send His armies down,
    To save and to sustain.

And in some gracious coming time
    Her banner white shall be,
The truest badge of might sublime
    That waves to land or sea.
And war's red-lettered creed die out
    Beneath her flowers of spring,
And when our martyrs fight and bleed,
    Their babes shall sit and sing.

TRUE TO THE LAST!

BY COL. W. S. HAWKINS, C. S. A.

A young officer, just before a fierce battle, wrote on the plating of his scabbard the address of his 'Ladye-love,' and the words, 'In the face of death my thoughts are thine.' He was killed; but a thoughtful comrade bore to her the sad memento of his fidelity.

The bugles blow the battle-call,
    And thro' the camp each stalwart band
To-day in serried columns forms,
    To fight for God and native land.

Brave men are marching by my side,
   Our banners floating glad and free,
But yet, amid these brilliant scenes,
   I give my thoughts to thee.

The horsemen dashing to and fro,⁵
   The drums with wild and thunderous roll,
The sights, the sounds, all things that tend
   To kindle valor in the soul.
These all are here, but in the maze
   Of squadrons moved with furious glee,
Still true to every vow we make,
   I give my thoughts to thee.

The deep booms smite the trembling air,
   Each throb proclaims the foeman near,
And proudly echoed from the front,
   I hear my gallant comrades cheer ;
Wild joy of heroes marching on,
   Thro' tears and blood their land to free—
I give to 'God and right' my life,
   But all my thoughts to thee.

And yet, beloved, I must not think
   What undreamed bliss may soon be mine,
It would unman me in the work
   Of guarding well my country's shrine.
Here on this sword I write my truth—
   These words may yet my solace be—
They'll tell how in this last fierce hour
   My thoughts were given to thee.

Along the east the holy morn
   Renews life's many cares and joys ;
This hour I hope some wish for me
   Thy pure and tender prayer employs.
Another beauteous dawn of light
   These eyes, alas ! may never see,
But even dying, faint, and maimed,
   I still would think of thee !

And then, in coming years that roll,
  When scenes of peace and brightness throng,
And round each happy hour is twined
  The wreaths of Friendship, Love and Song—
Go to his grave whose heart was thine,
  And by that spot a mourner be ;
One tear for him !—thy loved and lost—
  Whose last thoughts clung to thee !

SONNETS ON PICTURES.

BY COL. W. S. HAWKINS, C. S. A.

'THE DISARMING OF CUPID.'—*Correggio.*

Ho, Love ! thou pretty wanderer, thus I hold thee,
  And thus I take away thy shafts and bow ;
And here with fond and clinging arms enfold thee.
  Wee archer ! do not pout and threaten so.
Remember—thou wast ever woman's foe ;
  Not often thus hath maiden's might controlled thee '
Away ! thou peeping Satyr, there ! nor see
  The burning kiss I give my captive bold.
These arms shall now his dainty prison be—
  I clasp him here in warm luxurious fold !
Thou winsome happy god ! thy very sleep is lulled
  And fanned with zephyrs' perfume-laden breeze.
  Here rest thy cheek, in soft and rapturous ease,
On sweeter flower-beds than Graces ever culled.

'SAKONTALA.'—*Riedel.*

Most perfect form that ever roved the wild !
  Thou fond bright dream that comes from woodland
    bowers,
  Where thou hast played with doves, and shells, and
    flowers,
And taught the timorous fawn, and sung and smiled,

Till all kind faerie things have sought to bless
   Thy proud young life with gifts almost divine—
   Beads twinkle on thy limbs and wampums shine,
And pleads the soft-eyed deer for thy caress.
And thou art glad as light, and free as air !
   Taught that by streams and breezes unconfined,
   While I, pent up by gloomy bars that bind,
Can only dream of thee and freedom fair,
And sigh to be away, sweet daughter of the woods,
And rest for aye with thee, in shadowy solitudes.

SONNET TO MY SISTER 'COUNSELS.'

BY COL. W. S. HAWKINS, C. S. A.

I know, sister sweet, that no future of time
   Can bring to my strong heart the freshness of yore ;
But the oak of the autumn, in colors sublime,
   Is as grand as when hues of the spring it wore.
Then a goblet I quaff in captivity's gloom,
   And from flowers of fancy a circlet entwine,
A health and a garland to thee in thy bloom,
   While roses shall blow, while the grape yields
      wine ;
For however dark over me storms may enfold,
Thy life-light shall touch them with purple and gold.

A LETTER TO A FRIEND.

BY COL. W. S. HAWKINS, C. S. A.

Dear friend, at first I thought a song to weave,
Of daintiest rhymes, and measure low and sweet,
And wert thou but a little rustic maid,
Would still such posy lay beside thy feet;

But to thy worth should come some poet proud,
Whose soul's creative eye all things obey,
To touch his gorgeous instrument with joy,
And dedicate to thee the royal lay :
The winter-world of late has given way,
And earth puts forth the beauteous golden things
She dreamed of in the cold and starry nights,
And even the lone prisoner's life delights
To charm with May's sweet smile, and June's bright
      wings.
So to the winter of my heart, fair one,
Thy smile has brought the spring-time's touch of might,
And potent, like the day-dawn's glance of light,
Beneath *thy* influence the slow hours run—
Like some bright stream that plays and flashes o'er
The radiant plane of an opal floor,
Whose twinkling gems vie with the gorgeous sun ;
And all my *answering* life springs up in power,
And finds no longer any darkness lower ;
The branches bare, put forth with bud and bloom.
And, grateful, breathe their delicate perfume,
And slowly, sweetly grows their perfect flower.
I walk as in a clime of pleasant eves—
No objects there displease—no discord grieves ;
And even fainting hopes, their light relieves.
Thy picture is the April to this May—
The rosy dawn precedes the splendrous day.
Thy beauteous semblance here before me lies ;
The noble queen-like brow, the tender eyes ;
The rich and flossy bands of braided hair,
The shapely neck, so soft, and round, and fair ;
Half seen, the sly and modest little ear
Beneath concealing tresses gathered there,
Save one sweet cunning curl that strays and slips,
And down the white shoulder casts its wee eclipse.
Ah ! as I gaze, what voiceless longings come,
And *fondest prayers* fly to thee in thy home ;
A maiden's innocent and gentle bower,

Where birds their thrilling songs pipe every hour.
Where hope and love have built their tender shrine,
And everything seems pure and half divine —
A lovely garden-spot, and *thou* its flower !
My wish to come is vain, for prison-bars
Shut out my hope—but not the peerless stars
Which crowd the dome above us both to-night,
And gaze with sad and solemn eyes of light.
May flying cares but dim thy life's fair face,
As floating shadows dusk a limpid lake ;
' Mi Consuelo,' sparkling bird of grace,
Sit at my heart's wide-open lattice, take
At once thy theme and dwelling there—and move—
A light 'mid shade ! a star my clouds above !
Receive the fulness of thy brother's love.

AN INVOCATION.

BY COL. W. S. HAWKINS, C. S. A.

Come, thou sweet friend, and cheer awhile
    The brooding gloom of prison walls,
    Where thought depressed to sorrow calls,
And even joy forgets to smile.

Five weary moons have waxed and waned
    Since I was free—you know how free—
    I hardly dreamed such time would be
Ere I once more my hopes had gained.

Five dullest moons, in which I saw
    The winter pause in northward flight,
    Spread seven times his robe of white,
And then give way to April-thaw.

Next came the hours when earth was green
    You said, for these sad eyes could not
    See anywhere a garden plot,
Or look on any sylvan scene.

G 2

Then April, tired of sun and shower,
  Awoke the fair and lissom May,
  In bosky dell she slumberous lay,
And every feature seemed a flower!

With smiles she came, and blithe birds sang,
  And so a myriad swelling throats
  Poured forth their chime of grateful notes,
And with sweet thrills the woodlands rang.

And next was June, in stately pride,
  Love's countersign she knoweth well,
  She is Time's fairest sentinel,
With ruddy cherubs by her side ;

Than dainty May, more strong, more dear—
  To prouder truer glories born—
  The ripening fruit, the springing corn,
June is my month of all the year.

Your life with pleasure ripples now,
  For you can go each dewy morn—
  Spring's fairest picture you adorn—
And watching o'er the mountain's brow,

Can see earth deck her graceful form,
  And, bride-like, don her best array
  To meet her winsome lord—the day ;
And all her face, with blushes warm,

Mantles and glows to perfect life
  As the sunlight swells with radiant surge,
  And from your mind sweet thoughts emerge—
Your mind with fond love-thinkings rife.

'Tis yours to see the great trees toss
  Their heads and sportiveness employ,
  And shake at every gust, with joy,
Their broad leaves flecked with green and gloss.

And you can hear the jubilant strain,
 When tuneful bird, on wing that whirs,
 The summer's drowsy stillness stirs,
And throbbing echoes sing again.

And watch the days in joy arrayed,
 Each tripping coyly in its path,
 Like Beauty, dripping from her bath,
Far seen thro' woodlands' glinting shade.

'Tis yours to linger by the stream,
 And, looking in the pool's deep breast,
 To see your beauties all confest,
How like indeed to poet's dream!

'Tis yours, my glorious passion-flower!
 At this sweet season to appear,
 Like maiden from enchanted mere,
And bless for me each tardy hour.

So rose a Dryad from the wave,
 That parted to her rounded form,
 And soothed with loveliness the storm,
And to the fount new beauties gave.

So some magician's mystic might,
 Evoked from out his mirror's face
 A shape so luminous with grace,
That all his darkened room was light.

There is no gracious Dryad here,
 Nor have I mirror, wondrous fine,
 But I have thee, sweet friend of mine,
To bless me with thy influence dear.

'Tis mine, through thee, to see the spring,
 And feel its odorous, happy thrills;
 With thee go up the wooded hills,
And hear the choirs of Nature sing.

But no such scenes my vision greet,
  Pent up where glares the white-washed wall,
  Where summer's sultriest glances fall,
And barred is all the beaten street.

O narrow walk ! how oft the tread
  Of captive forms that knew no rest,
  On all your grassless length has prest,
And every step kept time to dread !

For here at silent hour of eve,
  And in the depth of starless gloom,
  Dead hopes come forth from out their tomb,
The prisoner's haunted heart to grieve.

O bounded sky ! what weary eyes
  A thousand times have looked to you,
  As with each slow hour trouble grew,
And life put on a sombre guise !

Ah ! deep and distant skies of June !
  Which erst I saw when I was free;
  Why come ye not once more to me,
With gorgeous sun and tender moon ?

'Tis not your sky, my June, that bends
  Above me now its narrow arc,
  Whose very brightness seemeth dark,
Whose noonday gleam with midnight blends.

For here there sings no summer bird,
  No sights of dewy freshness come ;
  No flowers smile, no wild bees hum,
E'en fancy's face with tears is blurred.

Here gloom and glee make wondrous strife,
  The brightest days are cast with cloud ;
  The budding hope soon finds a shroud,
And sorrow ploughs the fields of life.

Tho' in the past I bind my sheaves,
  The songs of olden time are missed,
  No ivory keys with fingers kissed,
For memory all my music weaves.

Life's first sweet notes for me are gone,
  As by the sea some wandering child
  Goes near the surges, lashing wild,
And seeks with eagerness the tone

That thrilled with joy his dreamy ear,
  But only finds the curling wave
  And whispering shell—his music's grave—
And lures its sigh, so far, so near.

Then, lost in that faint phantom charm—
  The elfin-sounds of nevermore !—
  Tho' dangerous billows beat the shore,
Stands heedless of their power to harm.

And yet some pleasures still remain,
  For even in this living tomb
  Some joys their little lights relume,
And fainting hopes rise firm again.

For when I hear each thundering gun,
  That shakes Virginian forests far,
  Where whilom friends in fury war,
Each throb to me seems victory won.

I think of volleying musketeers
  That form along the Georgian vales,
  Where no heart quakes, no spirit fails,
And fling away my qualmish fears.

I see the conflict nearly o'er,
  Where brother smites the brother down;
  Where all the air with death is sown,
And all the earth is wet with gore.

So after many a weary day,
   Some swimmer in the swirling sea,
   Where only skies and surges be
Through the horizon seen, and gray,

Sees break at last 'neath gradual morn.
   Just as his strength almost gives out,
   And jeering ocean-creatures shout,
And in him ghastly fear is born ;

Sees far away the dim shore line
   Over the hurtling waters loom,
   And all his being bursts in bloom
As forests wave and cities shine !

And almost hears each hurrying friend,
   With eager questionings of the lost,
   So long by crested billows tost—
And shouts of joy the zenith rend !

Thus I revive, but feel, dear one,
   That whether on the land or sea,
   And I in camp or prison be,
Thy star shall shine till life is done.

Come, then, and tint these darker days,
   And let each sun in gold go down;
   Come, crown me with thy friendship's crown,
And take these words of feeble praise.

Touch all my life with thy soft kiss—
   At that high thought the shadows fly,
   And fostering it, I feel that I
Thy form in heavenly courts would miss.

' Mi Consuelo,' true and bright,
   When thou art gone my peace is furled,
   And daylight shuts away the world,
And round me falls the brooding night.

'Tis thine to ease this crown of thorn,
  And pour some wine in misery's cup,
  Help weak hope build her towers up,
And light my prison-world with morn !

And when the immortal shore we tread,
  Together shall we join our strains,
  Together roam those shining plains
Where God's eternal peace is shed.

Camp Chase, Ohio:
  June 16, 1864.

LINES ON THE DEATH OF LIEUTENANT JOHN B. BOWLES.

BY FLORENCE ANDERSON.

Never again ! ah, never again
Shall he march proudly o'er the plain,
With head erect and flashing eye,
Bravely to conquer or to die.
No more—the stately head is low,
The blood-red tide has ceased to flow ;
The eye which burned with glory's fire,
The heart which throbbed with patriot ire,
Are senseless now to mortal pain,
They ne'er shall glow nor beat again.

He's dead. Alas ! so very fair ;
Push back the glossy waves of hair,
Wipe off the blood-stains from his brow,
Pure, cold and pale as marble now.
Never again, ah! never more !
His feet have touched the unknown shore,
His earthly course of glory's run,
Which we had fancied just begun.
One more brave heart in death is cold,
One more young form beneath the mould.

Oh, cruel war ! how thou dost come
To snatch the treasure from each home !
The dearest from each heart is torn,
The South doth mourn for her first-born.
God pity her : each day doth bring
For her increase of suffering.
What dearer sacrifice to truth
Than this brave, noble, generous youth ?
Loved with a love more sweet than fame,
Rich in the glory of a stainless name,
His spirit set amid the storms of war,
To rise in heaven a bright unfading star.

ON THE DEATH OF BRIGADIER-GENERAL CHARLES H. WINDER, OF MARYLAND.

By J. R. TRIMBLE, Major-Gen. C. S. A.

General Winder was killed by a cannon-shot in the battle of Slaughter's Mountain, Va., June 9, 1862. He was, at the time, in command of Jackson's 'Stonewall division.' He was an unpretending but a sincere and trusting Christian. He was a just, kind, faithful, noble gentleman. No one knew him but to respect, love, and honour; and no less the death of such a Christian, soldier, and gentleman, could have drawn a tear from Jackson's eye; a tribute which proclaimed his virtues more touchingly than the most plaintive requiem, or the proudest epitaph, for it needs but to say, 'Here lies one for whom Jackson shed a tear.'

The fight is o'er, the victory's won,
    We pause to count its cost ;
How many gallant, noble sons
    Of freedom have been lost !

They sleep with honors rudely paid,
    In chance and hasty graves,
And over Winder's manly head
    A lonely elm-tree waves.

'Oh! weep not for the fleetness
    That closed his brief career,
For memory sheds a sweetness
    All fragrant round his bier.'

And never cloud with sadness
    A name to honor given,
For hope, and faith, and gladness,
    Revealed his path to heaven.

And hope, and faith, and glory,
    Spoke in his parting cheer—
No Bayard famed in story
    Had less 'reproach and fear.'

'When he has found that higher sphere
    Where faith her Sabbath keeps,'
Shall those he loved let fall one tear?
    'He is not dead but sleeps.'

Though distant in their humble bed
    His lifeless relics lie,
Though 'dust to dust'—he is not dead—
    For virtues never die.

He climbed the steep of glory,
    Where laurel greenest grows;
And gives a name to story,
    While fame her trumpet blows.

Yet hearts will bleed, and gloom will shade
    The spirit's dream, when death
Strikes down in peace or warrior's blade,
    The noblest forms of earth.

Aye, tears *will* fall, and sadly
    Each heart bows down in pain;
E'en Jackson's eye is moistened
    With sorrow for the slain.

Thus tears appeal to heaven,
   Where greenest hopes turn sere ;
Yet, honor to the dead is given
   Where Jackson sheds a tear.

Hope dries each eye, for God
   ' Doth mark the sparrow's fall,
So surely he appoints the grave,
   And time to die '—for all.

Then, weep not for the fleetness
   That closed his brief career,
For memory sheds a sweetness
   And fragrance o'er his bier.

His warrior march was stainless, glorious, brief,
   He camps ' at rest,' 'neath Slaughter's Mountain
      shade—
His pilgrim soul now serves another chief,
   'Mid shining courts, with ' pearl and gold inlaid.'

Johnson's Island :
    September 1864.

WEEP ! WEEP !

BY ' REFUGEE.'

Weep ! weep ! for a fallen land,
   For a standard sheet laid low ;
Freedom is lost ! let every heart
   Echo the note of woe !
Yea, weep, ye soldiers, weep !
   'Twill not your manhood stain
To mourn with grievous bitterness
   Honor and valor slain.

Weep, friendless women, weep
   For the golden days of yore—
For the desolate homes, the aching hearts,
   The loved ones now no more ;

Bravely they fought and well,
  That noble hero band—
Bravely they fought and bravely died,
  To save their suffering land.

Our Southern soil is red
  With the blood of many slain;
Like sacrificial wine it fell,
  But the sacrifice was vain.
Peace dawns upon our land—
  O Heaven! that it should be
That Peace should smile o'er Freedom's grave,
  And we the smiles should see!

Let Southern men now take
  A long farewell to fame;
Let Southern men bow meekly down
  To tyranny and shame!
O Heaven! that such should live
  To hail the fatal hour
That crushes Freedom to the dust
  'Neath Northern hate and power!

But many a patient heart
  Yet thrills to the war-god's breath,
And many still would battle on
  For Freedom to the death!
Weep! weep! but not for them,
  The martyrs 'neath the sod,
For they *eternal* peace have found
  Around the throne of God!

Peace! Peace! 'tis but a word—
  A mockery—a name!
Alas, alas! 'tis but the wreath
  That hides the tyrant's chain:
And if it thus must be,
  And Freedom ne'er be won,
Then, Father! give us strength to say,
  Thy will on earth be done.

May 1865.

THE BROKEN SWORD.

BY M. W. M.

Suggested by an incident which occurred after the surrender
of Fort Donaldson.

No; never shall this trusty glaive,
   Which I so long have borne,
Be grasped by hands less true or brave,
   Or coward's side adorn.

Too oft in war its silver beam
   True men have followed far,
As thro' the battle-storm its gleam
   Flashed like a falling star.

Dear hands have bound it to my side;
   While struggling to repress
Unbidden tears, the sweet lips cried,
   Go, love; thy cause is blest!

And often in his childish joy,
   Along the shining blade,
The dimpled fingers of my boy
   In artless wonder strayed.

Then, think you I could lightly fling,
   At some proud foeman's feet,
A sword round which rich memories cling,
   So sacred, and so sweet.

No, rather let it evermore
   Rest 'neath thy rolling flood,
O stream, that laves my native shore,
   Now darkly stained with blood!

Then, proudly turning from them, he,
　　Unsheathing as he spoke
Its hallowed blade, across his knee
　　The tempered steel he broke.

And far into the azure stream
　　The glittering fragments threw,
And sternly watched their last faint gleam
　　Sink glimmering from his view.

Whate'er he felt, in tear or sigh,
　　Not there he sought relief—
It was not for a foeman's eye
　　To gaze upon *his* grief.

Roll on, thou river ! glad and free,
　　For ever pure and deep ;
A stainless hand has given to thee
　　A holy trust to keep !

Thou may'st have treasures rich and rare
　　Beneath thy restless wave ;
But none so precious can'st thou bear
　　As that true soldier's glaive!

TOO GOOD TO BE LOST.

The following lines were found written on the back of a five
hundred dollar Confederate note.

Representing nothing on God's earth now,
　　And naught in the water below it,
As a pledge of the nation that's dead and gone,
　　Keep it, dear friend, and show it—

Show it to those who will lend an ear
　　To the tale that this paper can tell,
Of liberty born, of the patriot's dream—
　　Of the storm-cradled nation that fell.

Too poor to possess the precious ores,
    And too much of a stranger to borrow,
We issued to-day our promise to pay,
    And hoped to redeem on the morrow.

The days rolled on, and weeks became years,
    But our coffers were empty still ;
Coin was so rare that the Treasury quaked
    If a dollar should drop in the till.

But the faith that was in us was strong, indeed,
    And our poverty well discerned ;
And these little checks represented the pay
    That our suffering volunteers earned.

We knew it had hardly a value in gold,
    Yet as gold our soldiers received it ;
It gazed in our eyes with a promise to pay,
    And each patriot soldier believed it.

But our boys thought little of price or pay,
    Or of bills that were over-due ;
We knew if it brought us bread to-day,
    It was the best our poor country could do.

Keep it, it tells our history all over,
    From the birth of its dream to the last ;
Modest, and born of the angel Hope,
    Like the hope of success it passed.

NUTS TO CRACK FOR COUSIN SAM.

BY JANET HAMILTON.

Have ye come to your senses yet, Sammy, my man,
For ye was just red-mad when the war it began ;
Hae the bluid ye hae lost, an' the physic ye've ta'en,
No cooled doun your fever, an' sobered your brain ?

What is't ye hae won?   Is it conquest an' fame?
Is't honor an' glory—a conqueror's name?
Is't the South wi' its cottons, an' planters, an' slaves?
It's nane o' them a'—it's a million o' graves.

What is't ye hae lost?   It's the big dollar-bags—
An' ye've naught in your pouches but dirty green
    rags ;
O' the hale o' your men naught is left but their
    banes,
An' the kintra is fu' o' their widows an' weans !

An' they've gaggit your press, an' they've steekit your
    mou,'
An' they've set the red mark o' auld Cain on your
    brow ;
An' the bairns o' your bairns that are yet to be born
Will be harried in taxes an' put to the horn.

The hale warl's glowrin and wonnerin what text
Your bluid-drinkin' parsons will open on next :
To Beecher and Brownlow I'll just say the word
Christ said to bauld Peter—'twas, ' Put up the
    sword.'

Aye, 'put up the sword,' an' hae done wi' your game :
Ye hae lost a' the stakes that ye played for—gang
    hame !
Look after your farm, let your neebours alane—
Ye hae work on your han,' or I'm muckle mistaen.

    Langloan.

TO THE VICTOR BELONG THE SPOILS.

BY M. W. M.

The following lines were suggested by the edifying spectacle of an officer exhibiting publicly on the cars, to his delighted wife, a carpet sack filled with silver plate robbed from Southern homes, and marked with the owners' names.

Oh, twine me a garland of laurel, my love !
   To rest and recruit from my wounds,
From the red battle-fields of the South I have come,
   All loaded with glory—and spoons.

I have brought you the trophies of many a fight,
   The relics of many a raid.
See, here are rich jewels that once sparkled bright
   On the form of some fair Southern maid.

And goblets of silver, all robbed from the hoard
   Of some haughty old double F. V.,
That often have shone on his family board,
   But now they may glitter for thee.

I thought of thee e'en in the midst of the strife,
   When a mansion was doomed to the fire ;
I held back the torch till I sought every room
   For something my love might desire.

I spared not the men in my wrath, and I thought
   As the women were rebels no less,
Tho' their blood it would not do to shed, I might take
   What they quite as much valued, ' I guess.'

So in spite of their tears, and entreaties, and threats,
   I ransacked their wardrobes and presses,
And bore off in triumph, to deck my fond bride,
   Such beautiful mantles and dresses.

No wonder you smile with delight, tho' the war
    To others brings sorrow and weeping ;
If it last but a little while longer, I vow,
    It will quite set us up in house-keeping.

We may even perhaps keep a carriage, and then
    My crest on the panels may shine—
'Bloody field,' with a spoon and fork crossed 'en argent,'
    While laurels around it entwine :

And the darkey I lured from his home in the South,
    As a coachman in livery shall go :
He is destitute here of both money and friends,
    And so will come *cheaply*, you know.

Then long may the 'star-spangled' banner wave on,
    And this 'cruel war' never be over ;
While plunder is plenty and patriots thrive
    On the spoils, we will 'live in the clover.'

VIRGINIA.

BY A VIRGINIA WOMAN.

'She leans on her spear to weep over her fallen heroes, but
its point is never lowered save at the breast of her foe.'

The mother of States ! In song and in story
    Virginia's the proudest name ever enrolled,
And freemen shall crown her with garlands of glory
    Whenever the tale of this contest is told.
Armed for the conflict, to her sisters she calls !
       Back, with her red right hand,
       Drives she that Northern band.
Do you pause ? Do you falter ? You are lost if she
    falls !

Proudly she waiteth the shock of the battle,
    Tho' her life-blood in torrents runs red on the plain ;
Where loud cannons roar and shrill muskets rattle,
    She has met them before, she must meet them again.

H 2

Armed for the conflict, to her sisters she calls !
> Back, with her red right hand,
> Drives she that Northern band !

Do you pause ? Do you falter ? You are lost if she
falls !

And see ! Where the Northern vulture hath fed
On hearts of her bravest, on heaps of her slain,
She kindles a pyre of light o'er the dead,
And leads her sons back to the battle again.
Armed for the conflict, to her sisters she calls !
> Back, with her red right hand,
> Drives she that Northern band !

Do you pause ? Do you falter ? You are lost if she
falls !

The homes of her children in ashes are laid,
The tears of her widows like fountains have run ;
They have wept for the homes where their children
have played,
They weep o'er the glory their husbands have won.
Armed for the conflict, to her sisters she calls !
> Back, with her red right hand,
> Drives she that Northern band !

Do you pause ? Do you falter ? You are lost if she
falls !

The heads of her mothers in sorrow have bowed
O'er the graves of their jewels. Like the Gracchi
of old,
Their jewels had souls. But they sleep in the crowd
Of heroes—none the less that their names are
untold.
Armed for the conflict, to her sisters she calls !
> Back, with her red right hand,
> Drives she that Northern band !

Do you pause ? Do you falter ! You are lost if she
falls !

To the 'Banquet of Death' she hath gathered each
    son ;
   Though her Jackson has fallen, Lee is still there !
There are battles to fight, there are fields to be won ;
   She yields not ! She shrinks not ! She will not
   despair.
Armed for the conflict, to her sisters she calls !
      Back, with her red right hand,
      Drives she that Northern band !
Do you pause ? Do you falter ? You are lost if she
   falls !

She trusts in her *birthright*, she trusts in her pride,
   And the swords of the children she would disen-
   thrall.
SHE TRUSTS THE GREAT CHIEFTAIN who stands by her
   side,
   And the faith of her fatherland—GOD OVER ALL.
Armed for the conflict, to her sisters she calls !
      Back, with her red right hand,
      Drives she that Northern band !
Do you pause ? Do you falter ? You are lost if she
   falls !

THE LAMENT.

BY A MISSOURIAN.

Where is the flag that once floated so proudly ?
Where the bright arms that once rang out so loudly ?
Where the brave hearts that so long held at bay
All the hosts of the North ? Where the jackets of
   gray ?
Chorus.
Down is the flag that once floated on high,
Low lie the hearts that would conquer or die ;
Sheathed are the swords that oft flashed in the van,
Lost is the cause of Truth, Freedom, and Man.

Hope has departed, life lost all its charms;
Our armies disbanded; oh! comrades in arms,
Taunted and *scorned* in our jackets of gray,
We may envy the brave souls who fell in the fray.

Lonely and weary the soldier returns,
Tells he's *paroled*, and his manly cheek burns.
Can life without liberty happiness yield?
Oh! would I had died on the red battle-field!

Hardships and toil for four long years endured,
Honor and triumphs by true hearts procured,
Now to be lost by poor cowards and knaves
Deserting their standard in haste to be slaves.

Hush, hush, my poor heart! be at ease, be at rest!
One comfort is mine, *that* the noblest and best:
I stood by our banner, I heard the last gun,
And can now say with pride, *I my duty have done.*

THE VANQUISHED PATRIOT'S PRAYER

Ruler of nations, bow Thine ear—
    I cannot understand
Thy ways; but Thou wilt heed this prayer
    For my beloved land.

Dear for young joys, and earnest toil
    Through many a stirring year;
My kindred blood has dyed her soil,,
    And made her trebly dear.

Teach me to sorrow with my land,
    Yet not to hate her foe—
To bow submissive to Thy hand,
    Which dealt the chastening blow.'

Withholden by Thy sovereign will
   What fain would I implore,
Give us some blessing richer still
   From out Thy boundless store.

Though now denied our blood-bought right,
   Yet grant us, Lord, to be,
In Thine and every nation's sight,
   Worthy of Liberty !

Pilgrims and strangers in the world—
   No land to call our own—
Our banner from its station hurled,
   Our Freedom from her throne ;

Let us not try, in scenes of mirth,
   For surcease from our grief ;
Help us to turn to heaven from earth—
   Seek there alone relief.

To suffer with a suffering race—
   Her bitter cup to share ;
Bear on that cross with patient face
   Which vanquished patriots bear.

Thus may heaven draw us more and more,
   Earth less entrancing be,
Until we reach the shining shore,
   And once again be free !

Dear fettered land ! this heart is given
   Till death, to thine and thee ;
When I forget thy woes, may heaven
   Cease to remember me.

THE RETURN HOME.

Aye, give them welcome home, fair South !
   For you they've made a deathless name ;
Bright through all after-time will glow
   The glorious record of their fame.
They made a nation !   What though soon
   Its radiant sun has seemed to set !
The *past* has shown what they can do,
   The *future* holds bright promise yet !

Philadelphia :
   July 1865.

THE SOUTH.

BY G.

Her head is bowed downwards ; so pensive her air,
   As she looks on the ground with her pale solemn
     face,
It were hard to decide whether faith or despair,
   Whether anguish or trust, in her heart holds a
     place.

Her hair was all gold in the sun's joyous light,
   Her brow was as smooth as the soft placid sea ;
But the furrows of care came with shadows of night,
   And the gold silvered pale when the light left the
     lea.

Her lips slightly parted, deep thought in her eye,
   While sorrow cuts seams in her forehead so fair ;
Her bosom heaves gently, she stifles a sigh,
   And just moistens her lid with the dew of a tear.

Why droops she thus earthward—why bends she?
    Oh, see !
  There are gyves on her limbs ! see her manacled
    hand !
She is loaded with chains, but her spirit is free,
  Free to love and to mourn for her desolate land.

Her jailer, though cunning, lacks wit to devise
  How to fetter her thoughts, as her limbs he has
    done ;
The eagle that's snatched from his flight to the skies,
  From the bars of his cage may still gaze at the sun.

No sound does she utter ; all voiceless her pains ;
  The wounds of her spirit with pride she conceals ;
She is dumb to her shearers ; the clank of her chains
  And the throbs of her heart alone tell what she feels.

She looks sadly around her ; how sombre the scene !
  How thick the deep shadows that darken her view.
The black embers of homes where the earth was so
    green,
  And the smoke of her wreck where the heavens
    shone blue.

Her daughters bereaved of all succor but God,
  Her bravest sons perished—the light of her eyes ;
But oppression's sharp heel does not cut 'neath the
    sod,
  And she knows that the chains cannot bind in the
    skies.

She thinks of the vessel she aided to build,
  Of all argosies richest that floated the seas,
Compacted so strong, framed by architects skilled,
  Or to dare the wild storm, or to sail to the breeze.

The balmiest winds blowing soft where she steers,
  The favor of heaven illuming her path;
She might sail as she pleased to the mild summer airs,
  And avoid the dread regions of tempest and wrath;

But the crew quarrelled soon o'er the cargo she bore;
  'Twas adjusted unfairly, the cavillers said;
And the anger of men marred the peace that of yore
  Spread a broad path of glory and sunshine ahead.

There were seams in her planks—there were spots on
      her flag,
  So the fanatics said, and they seized on her helm,
And from soft summer seas, turned her prow where
      the crag
  And the wild breakers rose the good ship to
  o'erwhelm.

Then the South, though true love to the vessel she
      bore,
  Since she first laid its keel in the days that were
      gone;
Saw it plunge madly on to the wild billows' roar,
  And rush to destruction and ruin forlorn.

So she passed from the decks, in the faith of her heart
  That justice and God her protectors would be;
Not dashed like a frail fragile spar, without chart,
  In the fury and foam of the wild raging sea.

The life-boat that hung by the stout vessel's side
  She seized, and embarked on the wide trackless
      main,
In the faith that she'd reach, making virtue her guide,
  The haven the mother ship failed to attain.

But the crew filled with wrath, and they swore by
    their might
  They would sink the brave boat that did buffet the
    sea,
For daring to seek, by her honor and right,
  A new port from the storms, a new home to be free.

So they crushed the brave boat; all forbearance they
    lost;
  They littered with ruins the ocean so wild,
Till the hulk of the parent ship, beaten and tossed,
  Drifted prone on the flood by the wreck of the child.

And the bold rower, loaded with fetters and chains,
  In the gloom of her heart sings the proud vessel's
    dirge;
Half forgets, in its wreck, all the pangs of her pains,
  As she sees its stout parts floating loose in the surge.

Savannah, Ga.:
  August 17, 1865.

THE CONFEDERATE FLAG.

No more o'er living hearts to wave,
  Its tattered folds for ever furled;
We laid it in an honored grave,
  And left its memories to the world.

The agony of long, long years
  May in a moment be compressed,
And with a grief too deep for tears
  A nation's heart may be oppressed.

Oh! there are those who die too late
  For faith in God, and Right and Truth—
The cold mechanic grasp of Fate
  Hath crushed the roses of their youth.

More blessed are the dead who fell
    Beneath it in unfaltering trust,
Than we who loved it passing well
    Yet live to see it trail the dust.

It hath no future which endears,
    And this farewell shall be our last:
Embalm it in a nation's tears,
    And consecrate it to the past,—

To mouldering hands that to it clung,
    And flaunted it in hostile faces,—
To pulseless arms that round it flung
    The fervor of their last embraces,—

To our dead heroes—to the hearts
    That thrill no more to love or glory,—
To those who acted well their parts,
    Who died in youth, and live in story.

With tears for ever be it told,
    Until oblivion covers all;
Until the heavens themselves wax old
    And totter slowly to their fall.

PEACE—TO THE DEAD ALONE!

BY A SOUTHERN LADY.

They are ringing Peace on my heavy ear,
    No Peace to this heavy heart—
They are ringing Peace. I hear—I hear—
    O God! how my hopes depart!

They are ringing Peace from the mountain side,
    With a hollow voice it comes;
They are ringing Peace o'er the sea-girt tide,
    While the billows sweep our homes.

They are ringing Peace, and the spring time blooms
   Like a garden fresh and fair ;
But our martyrs sleep in their silent tombs,
   Do they *hear* ?   O God ! do they *hear* ?

They are ringing Peace, and the battle-cry
   And the bayonet's work are done,
And the armor bright they are laying by
   From the brave sire to the son !

And the musket's clang, and the soldier's drill,
   And the tattoo's nightly sound,
We shall hear no more with a joyous thrill—
   Peace, Peace, they are ringing around !

There are women *still* as the stifled air
   On the burning desert's track—
Not a cry of joy, not a welcome cheer,
   And their brave sons coming back !

There are fair young heads in their morning pride,
   Like the lilies, pale they bow,
Just a memory left to the soldier's bride—
   God help—God help them now !

There are martial steps that we may not hear,
   There are forms that we may not see—
Death's muster-roll they have answered clear—
   They are *free*—thank God, *some are free* !

Not a fetter fast, nor a prisoner's chain,
   For the noble army gone,
No conqueror comes in the heavenly plain—
   Peace, Peace to the *dead* alone !

They are ringing Peace, but strangers tread
   O'er the land where our fathers trod,
And our birthright joys, like a dream, have fled,
   And Thou—where art Thou, O God !

They are ringing Peace—*not here—not here*—
 Where the victor's march is set ;
Roll back to the North its mockery cheer,
 No Peace to the South-land yet !

May 1865.

COLUMBIA.

BY J. C. J.

On thy banks, in pride and beauty,
 Stands the city, Congaree !
And a whole State's love and duty
 Centres in, Columbia, thee !
Where the waters, ever shifting,
 Break in rapids bold and free—
To the sky thy towers uplifting,
 Thou sit'st a queen upon the lea !

In the autumn's early mornings,
 In the splendid days of spring,
At the summer's glorious dawnings,
 When the wings of winter bring,
Glistening on their tips, the hoar-frost,
 Glittering 'mid their plumes, the snow—
Thou wast lovely, O Columbia ! peaceful, happy
  too thou wast,
Ere the Vandal foemen's firebrand laid thee
  level with the dust !

Crowned with beauty, in all quiet
 Slept thy groves beneath the moon,
While the mock-bird's song ran riot
 In its vagaries of tune !
Ah ! how sore, how sad the change is !
 Where is all thy beauty now ?
Where ? oh, *where* ? alas ! how strange is
 Now the crown upon thy brow !

Dark and angry rolls the river,
　Fierce and loud the rapids roar!
Sad, and low, and mournful, ever
　Wash the eddies at the shore!

Where the mock-bird's notes enraptured,
　Chained, entranced, the listener's ear—
Where, from fairest flowers captured,
　Fragrance, floating, filled the air—
Where soft words of love were spoken—
　Where sweet vows of love were vowed,
And the quiet ne'er was broken
　By harsh notes of discord loud—
Where thy household gods and fires
　Soothed the sense, and charmed the eye—
Where thy proud and lofty spires
　Soaring upward pierced the sky—
All is burned! All! All is dreary!
　And the scorched and blackened trees,
Sob in mournful numbers, weary,
　To the sighing of the breeze!

THE SOUTHERN WIFE.

BY M. W. M.

A price is on my darling's head,
　Outlawed and hunted down;
Yet is my love more proudly true
　Than if it wore a crown.

A crown—thy dark hair is a crown,
　And if amid its curls
Gleam silver lines of care, they shine
　Fairer to me than pearls.

Vainly they strive to brand thy brow,
  That dauntless brow with shame ;
I never knew how proud till now
  I was to bear thy name.

My woman's heart swells with the thought
  And triumph fills my breast,
To know that fearless head had sought
  No other place of rest.

How blest a privilege to share
  A patriot's high career ;
There is no pang I could not bear
  For cause and love so dear.

For worlds I would not shame my lord
  With unavailing fears,
Nor gird my soldier with a sword
  Stained by a woman's tears.

I know that many a costly life
  Of father, husband, son,
Must yield in this wild battle-strife
  Ere all is lost or won.

Yet will I compass thee about
  Where'er thy footsteps move,
With the strong rampart of my prayers—
  The yearning prayers of love.

THEN AND NOW.

BY J. C. J.

The following was written on returning to my home, which
had been burned and desolated by Sherman's Army.

I saw a scene at sunrise,
  A year or two ago,
That filled my heart with joy as pure
  As ever soul might know.

I saw a quiet homestead,
　　Embowered in a grove
Of oaks, to which sweet flowering vines
　　Clung tenderly, with love.

I saw the varied flowers
　　All glittering with the dew,
Which melted in the rising light
　　To perfume rich and new.

I saw the mistress of the place—
　　Her soft brown eye, her brow,
Bespoke a soul all loveliness.
　　Methinks I see her now!

As with a stately step she passed,
　　And with a queenly air,
Amid the beauteous flowers and shrubs
　　Her taste had gathered there.

I saw her eye light up with joy
　　And pride, as round she glanced
Upon the beauties of the place
　　Her care had so enhanced.

For 'twas her soul's fixed, ardent wish
　　To leave this to her son
' A finished place,' whene'er the hours
　　Of her life's day were done.

And well she had succeeded;
　　It *was* ' a finished place.'
Beauty, comfort—all was there—
　　In all her hand you'd trace.

　　*　　*　　*　　*　　*

I saw a scene at sunset,
　　A day or two ago,
That gave my heart, my mind, my soul,
　　Unutterable woe!

I

The rain was falling thick and fast,
　　The clouds were drifting low ;
In unison my spirits seemed,
　　My step grew sad and slow.

I saw a grass-grown garden,
　　A crumbling pile of brick—
A vacant space where the homestead stood,
　　And dank weeds growing thick.

War's bloody sword, by Vandals waved,
　　Had glittered o'er the place ;
Of all its beauty, all its joy,
　　There was not left a trace !

Weeds had choked out the flowers
　　That greeted me before ;
The house was burned—the charm was gone—
　　The mistress was no more !

The foe's success had crushed her soul, ·
　　And this fresh anguish gave,
This wanton ruin of her place—
　　She *could* not live a slave.

No more !　And she—my *mother* ;
　　But words are vainly weak
In such a case—she sank to rest
　　A Christian, pure and meek.

AN INCIDENT OF THE WAR.

BY M. W. M.

On one occasion, during the war in Virginia, General Lee was lying asleep by the wayside, when an army of 15,000 men passed by, with hushed voices and footsteps, lest they should disturb his slumbers.

O'ercome with weariness and care,
　　The war-worn veteran lay
On the green turf of his native land,
　　And slumbered by the way.

The breeze that sighed across his brow,
   And smoothed its deepened lines,
Fresh from his own loved mountains bore
   The murmur of their pines,
And the glad sound of waters,
   The blue rejoicing streams
Whose sweet familiar tones were blent
   With the music of his dreams :
They brought no sound of battle's din,
   Shrill fife, or clarion,
But only tenderest memories
   Of his own fair Arlington ;
With, perhaps, a grander vision,
   Which, alas ! was not to be,
Of a new-born banner floating
   O'er a land redeemed and free.
While thus the chieftain slumbered,
   Forgetful of his care,
The hollow tramp of thousands
   Came sounding through the air ;
With ringing spur and sabre,
   And trampling feet they come,
Gay plume and rustling banner,
   And fife, and trump, and drum :
But soon the foremost column
   Sees where, beneath the shade,
In slumber, calm as childhood,
   Their wearied chief is laid ;
And down the line a murmur
   From lip to lip there ran,
Until the stilly whisper
   Had spread to rear and van ;
And o'er the host a silence
   As deep and sudden fell
As though some mighty wizard
   Had hushed them with a spell ;

And every sound was muffled,
  And every soldier's tread
Fell lightly as a mother's
  Round her baby's cradle-bed;
And rank, and file, and column,
  So softly on they swept,
It seemed a ghostly army
  Had passed him as he slept:
But mightier than enchantment
  Was that whose magic wove
The spell that hushed their voices—
  Deepest reverence and love.

GOING HOME.

BY M. L. M.

No flaunting banners o'er them wave,
  No arms flash back the sun's bright ray,
No shouting crowds around them throng,
  No music cheers their onward way;
They're going home!   By adverse fate
  Compelled their trusty swords to sheathe;
True soldiers they, even though disarmed—
  Heroes, though robbed of victory's wreath.

Brave Southerners! with sorrowing hearts
  We gaze upon them through our tears,
And sadly feel how vain were all
  Their heroic deeds through weary years;
Yet 'mid their enemies they move
  With firm, bold step and dauntless mien.
O Liberty! in every age
  Such have thy chosen champions been.

Going home!—alas! to them the words
  Bring visions fraught with gloom and woe.
Since last they saw those cherished homes,
  The legions of th' invading foe

Have swept, like the simoon, along,
  Spreading destruction far and wide.
' They found a garden, but they left
  A howling wilderness behind.'

Ah ! in those desolated homes
  To which ' the fate of war has come,'
Sad is the welcome, poor the feast,
  That wait the soldier's coming home.
Yet loving ones will round him throng,
  With smiles more tender, if less gay,
And joy will brighten pallid cheeks
  At sight of the *dear boys in gray.*

KENTUCKY.

BY ALETHEIA.

It is a time for action, not ' for memory and for
    tears ; '
Then hush this childish wailing, and banish craven
    fears.
The war-cloud's lurid lightning already round us
    plays,
And peace has now become a myth, a dream of
    bygone days.

A dream not gone for ever, but rudely banished
    now,
The cannon-roar at Charleston too surely tells us
    how ;
To ears so long accustomed to chiming Sabbath
    bells,
How fearfully portentous that deep, hoarse thunder
    swells.

'Tis not the knell of liberty, 'tis not the knell of
    truth,
'Tis not the funeral tolling for Columbia in her
    youth ;
But 'tis the voice of freemen, who never knew dis-
    grace,
Protesting against tyranny—Blair, Seward, Lincoln,
    Chase.

We who have known communion, so long a friendly
    band,
Must mourn the desolation that threatens our fair
    land ;
But let the tears not blind our eyes in the oncoming
    strife—
Without the crown of *honor*, there is no worth in life.

Our State has held the olive-branch, and humbly
    sued to those
Who, under name of brethren, have proved our dead-
    liest foes,
The suit was spurned, and now, ye winds ! proclaim
    the truth afar,
Kentucky was for union, but is not afraid of war.

The spirits of our gallant sires would rise could they
    but think
One of their brave descendants would from his duty
    shrink,
Or if they thought one dastard of all the number
    could
Give his consent to help to shed one drop of South-
    ern blood,

Or let his poor dependents, first cause of all the
    strife,
Who cling like very parasites, and draw from him
    their life,

His nurse, his children's playmates, companions of
    his toil,
Be sacrificed or yielded up, an envious foeman's
    spoil.

Have they no human memories to bind them to the
    sod
Where they have served their masters, and learned
    to worship God,
That they should be by tyrant power torn from each
    home and hearth,
To seek their former level, the lowest of the earth ?

No—we'll protect our negroes ; 'twould be a deep
    disgrace
To offer as a sacrifice this faithful, helpless race.
The God of freedom would refuse the offering were
    it made ;
He gives responsibilities which we cannot evade.

We'll be again for union, when union guarantees
Honor and truth and justice, and all our liberties,
But we are not for union when it is but a name,
A cloak for base hypocrisy—a noble freeman's
    shame.

    April 1861.

VIRGINIA, 1861.

Land of my birth ! my love, my pride, all honor to
    thy name,
Thy children have no cause to blush, though jealous
    of thy fame !
For thou art still tenacious of honor and of truth
As in the days, the glorious days, of thy historic
    youth !

The generous pride, the noble blood, the scorn of all
    things base,
Which time and chance and ruthless change are
    powerless to efface,
Still mark thee to the loyal heart as mother of the
    free,
Who raise their voice, like Henry, for ' Death or
    Liberty.'

Thou'rt proud, fair nurse of heroes ! but thou art
    justly so,
Cornelia of the nations ! for none like thee can show
A fadeless crown of honored names, where one a
    lustre sheds
More glorious than the diadems that deck earth's
    royal heads.

Thy children are thy jewels, and many more would
    shine
With yet a richer splendor in this precious crown of
    thine,
But all the lesser lights are paled, as stars before the
    sun,
By the unrivalled glory of thy peerless Washington.

War-clouds are gathering o'er thee now, but 'mid
    the coming storm,
Thy brave devoted children shall shield thee from all
    harm,
And we, who cannot wield the sword, may pray to
    God for thee,
That He will keep thee from the scourge of Northern
    tyranny.

Thy living sons will fight for thee, and in the view-
    less air
A spirit-host will circle thee, in answer to our
    prayer;

Thy heroes from the Elysian fields will point the
    avenging sword,
To scatter from thy hallowed soil the North's
    barbarian horde.

God keep thee, honored mother! by His own
    almighty power,
From the vengeance of the tyrant, in the battle's
    awful hour;
And grant that of thy children not one may live to
    see
The regal Old Dominion e'er bend the suppliant
    knee.

AFTER THE BATTLE OF BULL RUN.

Sadly and low,
Hear how the fitful breezes blow!
    They are sighing
    For many dying,
As the night-winds come and go.

Fearfully well,
A tale of woe these night-winds tell,
    A tale of horror—
    Oh! that the morrow
Could its fearfulness dispel.

O God! O God!
Dark crimson stains are on the sod,
    And the silvery Run,
    In the setting sun,
Is an artery filled with blood!

Roses are crushed,
With brothers' blood all darkly flushed.
    We have no sighs
    For the flower that dies,
So many hearts in death are hushed.

Oh, night-winds, moan !
So many hurried before God's throne,
All unshriven,
And unforgiven—
How can they meet the Judge alone ?

Soft angel-eyes,
Down from the midnight's cloudy skies,
Pour the rain
Till the crimsoned plain
Loses the stain of this sacrifice.

Draw close the pall
Of clouds and darkness over all.
Dying and dead
On their gory bed
Even the stoutest hearts appal !

A requiem low
Chant, ye pines ! as the night-winds blow !
The coming years
Will be full of tears,
And many hearts will break with woe.

July 21.

THE BATTLE OF MANASSAS.

' The bridal of the earth and sky,' the blessed Sab-
bath-morn,
Brightens into the perfect day from its soft, rosy
dawn ;
But ' Peace on Earth ' is not the cry borne on the
summer air,
And many, many beating hearts forget the hour of
prayer.

Upon the listening silence no mellow sound of bell
In long vibrating cadences will rise and sink and
    swell;
But discords to appal stout hearts, the cannon's thun-
    der-tones,
The rattling hail of musketry, the shrieks, the dying
    groans.

Our foes have forced it on us to desecrate this day,
They have come forth to conquer us in battle's stern
    array.
May God forgive the sacrilege, and by His mighty
    power
Sustain the cause of Right and Truth in this most
    trying hour.

See how yon plumed and marshalled host, in long
    and glittering lines,
Moves to the deeper shadows beneath the tall dark
    pines,
Remember, comrades, they have come to make our
    people slaves,
Remember 'tis your privilege to find them bloody
    graves.

This is the tide in your affairs, then take it at the
    flood,
The tide that leads to honor now must be the tide
    of blood.
Forward, brave columns! forward! to meet the host
    that comes,
With fire and sword, with murderous hands, to violate
    your homes.

Virginia to the earth's oppressed, from every dis-
    tant land,
Extends her hospitality with generous, friendly hand;

Virginia to the oppressor extends a point of steel,
Which in his deepest heart of hearts we'll make the
  invader feel.

Hark to the shout of victory! now nothing can
  withstand
The torrent-sweep, the stormlike rush, of that brave
  patriot band ;
The ranks are broke, the foemen fly, in wild confusion driven,
Like autumn leaves, or frightened birds, before the
  blasts of heaven.

Land of my love, Virginia! upon my bended knee,
I thank the God of battles who hath so succored
  thee.
The army of thy boasting foe is scattered and
  undone,
And by His help the victory most signally is won.

We'll raise the glad *Te Deum*; for God hath surely
  given,
To aid thy just and holy cause, the avenging wrath
  of heaven ;
And they who came to subjugate, o'erwhelm thee
  like a flood,
Have dyed thy silvery rivulets with their own gush-
  ing blood.

With blinded eyes and vengeful hearts they rushed
  to meet their fate.
How Southrons greet invaders they realise too late ;
Their hearts' life-blood in crimson tide sinks in the
  thirsting ground,
And many 'neath thy sacred soil dishonored graves
  have found.

But mingled with the victors' shout there is a wail
    of woe,
For lofty heads and gallant hearts in death are lying
    low ;
They left their flowery Southern homes to battle for
    the right—
They have fallen, but like heroes, in the thickest of
    the fight.

Green be their graves and bright their names in
    history's roll of fame,
Inheritance their country's sons would rather die
    than shame.
Their epitaphs we'll proudly write when our Southern
    land is free,
For they have struck at tyrant power, and died for
    liberty.

July 21, 1861.

MANASSAS RACES.

POPULAR NEWSPAPER VERSION.

' I think there be six Richmonds in the field.'

The mighty army of the North is whipped, and its
    remains
Are scattered in confusion o'er Virginia's sandy
    plains ;
The Ariel that beguiled the host (was ever sprite so
    tricksy ?)
Led them to hopeless shipwreck to the pretty tune of
    Dixie.

They wished them all in Dixie ; but when the host
    was ranged
'Fore Beauregard's ' masked batteries ' their tune
    was quickly changed ;

They wished them back in Washington ;—how could
    those rebels dare
To throw up such intrenchments, to take them in a
    snare ?

'Twas unpolite in Beauregard to block communica-
    tion
With Richmond, when 'the Army' made such
    mighty preparation.
And such a disappointment too! ah, me! it was a
    pity ;
The Zouaves all had set their hearts on visiting
    that city.

And General Scott! it will afflict the 'war-worn
    veteran' so,
That in his way his native State should such obstruc-
    tions throw ;
Octogenarian as he is, they ought not so to vex him,
In his bewildered state of mind 'twas cruel to
    perplex him.

And Mr. Lincoln, 'honest man!' to whom the
    nation's grateful,
Why should the 'Rebels,' to his mind, have made
    themselves so hateful ?
He only wished to send some friends to see their
    famous region ;
The Black Horse intercepted them and Colonel
    Hampton's Legion.

At Centreville the 'Rebels' ran—what disingenuous
    flattery !
'Twas but to lead 'the Army' on to some foul
    hidden battery,
And they of such deception were so wholly unsuspi-
    cious !
They did not think the 'Chivalry' could be so very
    vicious.

But when they saw the ' Chivalry ' had such a *ruse*
    employed,
The *officers* began to think *they* would not be
    decoyed,
But left the men to fight it out without their own
    assistance,
While they beheld the battle rage, at a convenient
    distance.

The men fought on, and after a while they thought
    without compunction
That they would soon be masters of the famed
    Manassas Junction ;
They raised the cup of victory—but between the cup
    and lip,
According to the adage, there has been many a slip.

Jeff. Davis came upon the field, on this they had not
    counted,
Like Death in the Apocalypse, on a pale horse he
    was mounted !
The superstitious teamsters then believed he was a
    ghost,
And so impressed it on the minds of all the Northern
    host.

Then not ' like heroes in the strife,' but like wild
    herds of cattle,
The teamsters struck across the plain, and left the
    field of battle ;
The Congress men next took the track with terror on
    their faces,
And gave convincing proof of speed at the Manassas
    Races.

The generals and the officers, who had been so
    delighted,
Now, like the valiant Congress men, began to be
    affrighted ;

Deserted by their gallant chiefs, 'the Army' was
    undone, sir,
So followed their example, and quickly 'cut and
    run,' sir.

Afraid the 'rebels' would pursue, each man as he
    receded,
With hat and coat, and musket too, the roads and
    lanes impeded,
The men who manned the cannon cut the horses from
    the traces,
To give the greater *éclat* to the famed Virginia Races.

Historians, with impartial eye, throughout all coming
    ages,
And those whom, like my idle self, the poet's rhyme
    engages,
Will scan the records of that flight in wondering
    admiration,
To mark the time 'the Army' made from the
    Manassas Station.

LINES ON THE PRESENTATION OF A CONFEDERATE FLAG.

Our banner hidden from the light of day,
Where tyrant minions hold a despot sway,
Shall in the freedom of the Southern land,
In the firm clasp of some true patriot hand,
Unroll its starry blazon to the light,
And bid you onward in the cause of right.

Guard it amid the battle's darkest hour,
Emblem of justice, of Confederate power!
Bear it aloft above the crimson plain,
Dyed with the welling heart's blood of the slain,
Proud let it wave in victory o'er each field,
And teach the foe we know not how to yield.

Kentucky's daughters, send this flag to those
Who'll bear it bravely 'gainst their Northern foes,
Who'll take away the mantling blush of shame
That rises at Kentucky's once-loved name,
And prove beneath a glowing Southern sky
For *right* Kentuckians *yet* will dare to die.

AN ADDITION TO THE BONNIE BLUE FLAG.

A tribute to true Kentuckians.

And we will add another cheer for our Kentucky
     State,
Her sons in this most glorious war have proved both
     brave and great ;
Her Breckinridge and Buckner and Morgan too have
     given
A glittering star that shines afar in the Confederate
     heaven.
   Hurrah ! hurrah ! for Southern rights, hurrah !
   Hurrah for the Bonnie Blue Flag that bears Ken-
     tucky's Star !

We'll raise no more the blush of shame on fair
     Kentucky's brow,
For she is with us heart and soul in every contest
     now ;
She gives her sons and gives her prayers to aid us in
     the war,
Then add unto the Bonnie Blue Flag the bright
     Kentucky Star.
   Hurrah ! hurrah ! for Southern rights, hurrah !
   Hurrah for the Bonnie Blue Flag that bears Ken-
     tucky's Star !

K

TO KENTUCKIANS.

On the Dispersion of the Convention at Frankfort by
Col. Gilbert.

If in your ' ashes live their wonted fires,'
If ye are sons of your heroic sires,
Kentuckians! while the tide of battle rolls,
Wake from the lethargy that wraps your souls,
And each man gird his sword upon his thigh,
Resolved to conquer, or like men to die.

Oh! what is life if bought with all men prize,
Or ease secured by honor's sacrifice?
Kentuckians! you should scorn like slaves to lie
In the base bonds of this foul tyranny,
While your own brethren, in each ghastly fight,
Do gallant battle for the cause of right.

Go---e'er it be too late to save your fame,
Brand from the burning of undying shame,
Go—leave your lands, your houses, and your wives,
Go—reverently offer up your lives,
Atone the wrong you've done the Southern cause—
Avenge the insults offered to your laws.

Never before was such appeal in vain!
If woman's tears could free you from the stain—
If woman's voice in council had been heard—
If woman's strength sufficed to wield the sword—
Kentucky never would have bowed so low
To do obeisance to a dastard foe!

Look at Virginia, your own mother State,
Learn from her sons how to be truly great!
Her Ashby, Stuart, Jackson, Longstreet, Lee,
Her proud array of princely chivalry!
Have they no power to raise your slumbering sense
And make you long for virtue's recompense?

Why not resist the brutal tyrant-stroke ?
Why bow your necks so tamely to his yoke ?
Have you lost power to feel the sting of shame ?
Do you count honor nothing but a name ?
Has fame no guerdon—victory no wreath—
That you would snatch e'en from the jaws of death ?

Oh ! do not blindly court a hideous fate !
Wake ! ere it be eternally too late.
Rise ! break the cords with which they hope to chain
This Samson till his mighty soul is slain.
Rise ! bring confusion to the treacherous foe,
And lay his boasting pride and malice low !

Alas ! alas ! that we should live to see
This land no longer worthy to be free !
Men born to your proud heritage of fame
Content to forfeit their chivalrous name—
Content to lose all but the paltry gold
For which their birthright has been basely sold !

STONEWALL JACKSON.

In Memoriam.

Oh ! weep ; our gallant chief's among the dead !
Cold lies the sod above his noble head,
Heavy the dull reluctant earth is pressed
Upon our hero's gentle, faithful breast.
Virginia mourns this well-beloved one,
Her tried, and true, and patriotic son,
Him, numbered now among the gallant dead,
Him, round whose name a glorious light is shed,
A light to brighten through all coming time,
As men shall read his character sublime.

Can pride in him now quench the burning tear,
Or fame console for loss of one so dear ?
No ; they but stir the heart, and make it know
The deepest anguish of bereavement's woe.

Well may the nation mourn, he was a part
Of the great people's idolising heart;
His fame was theirs, his greatness was their boast;
Others they prized, but *him* they *loved* the most.
And he is dead! and did not live to see
The consummation of that liberty
Which he had counted worthy this great strife,
For which he offered up his peerless life!

Hero of heroes! true, austere, and pure!
The memory of thy virtues shall endure
Until all hearts shall kindle into flame,
Caught from the matchless glory of thy name,
Freedom shall beacon nations from thy tomb,
There sound the knell of despotism's doom,
For thou did'st dare to fill a freeman's grave,
But could'st not stoop to be the tyrant's slave!

Thou'st writ thy name on history's living page,
Thou'st left thy country such a heritage,
Thou'st been God's instrument to shield her so,
To guard her from so many a cruel blow,
The weight of obligation might oppress
Were it conferred by one we reverenced less.
O South! baptized in blood, and woman's tears,
Cherish the fame, through all thy future years,
Of him who now is hallowed unto thee
By death's divine and awful mystery!

Bold unto rashness, true to freedom's cause,
Swift to avenge our desecrated laws,
Modest and pure, a valiant Christian knight,
Ready to die 'for God and for the Right,'
A man whose foemen were constrained to yield
The glory won on many a hard-fought field,
And while they envied, yet could not control
Their admiration of that rare, grand soul,
Which shone, like freedom's bright and constant star,
Above the dark and threatening clouds of war.

The sword has fallen from the nerveless hand,
The chieftain leads no more his chosen band!
No more, ' appealing from his native sod,'
Will prayer and supplication rise to God,
No more his fury on the foeman fall,
No more the terror of his name appal!
The strife is o'er, the mighty soul is fled,
Our ' deathless hero ' numbered with the dead.
Yet, though unfilled the measure of his fame,
He leaves his country's proudest boast, *his fame.*

May 20, 1863.

MY NATIVE LAND.

Where is my Native Land ?
Not on Kentucky's conquered soil,
Where hireling hordes her wealth despoil ;
Where men are bound in willing chains,
And naught of liberty remains ;
Where all are dead to honor, fame,
And woman weeps o'er manhood's shame.
Thank God it is not here.

Not on this ' dark and bloody ground,'
Where honesty no more is found,
Where every spark of valor's dead,
And justice from her seat is fled,
Debased, corrupt, despised and jeered,
Her power, her wrath, no longer feared.
Thank God it is not here.

Not here, where in religion's fanes
Instead of God the despot reigns,
Where priests give thanks for blood that pours
From Maryland to Texas' shores,
And use religion's awful might
To crush in men the sense of right.
Thank God it is not here.

Where is my Native Land ?
'Tis on Virginia's glorious sod,
Where man bows only to his God,
Where justice rules with temperate power
The struggling nation's darkest hour,
Where men, the tried, the true, the brave,
Have died their liberties to save.
    There is my Native Land.

Where valor makes a desperate stand,
And, fighting, falls with sword in hand,
Where every river, mountain, plain,
Is red with battle's crimson stain,
Where woman sheds no burning tear
Above her sons' dishonored bier.
    There is my Native Land.

Where men of honor have had birth,
Who shine among the great of earth,
Statesmen, a long and proud array,
Chieftains, the first in battle's fray,
Heroes, above ambition's aim,
Have given to thee undying fame,
    My own dear Native Land.

Admired, revered, Virginia's name
Awakes no kindling blush of shame !
My deepest heart with longing yearns,
My freeborn soul with ardor burns
To read the deeds of valor done,
The battles fought, the glory won,
    By thee, my Native Land.

December 1864.

SONGS OF THE SOUTH

AND

OTHER POEMS.

BY KENTUCKY.

————◆————

Dedicated to KENTUCKY'S DEAD, who lie on every Southern battlefield and in the graveyard of every United States prison ; — To those sworn into the Confederate service who have been foully murdered as guerillas ; —and To those who have been shot on their way to the C.S.A., or in attempting an escape from Northern prisons that they might again fight for their beloved South.

————

' My son has said, what vexes one, that one must labor of ; and when he had a grief he made a poem of it.'—GOETHE'S MOTHER.

CONFISCATION.

A WIFE TO HER HUSBAND.

Let us go forth into the cold, cold snow!
A tyrant says we must, or bow us low
    At sound of his decree.
Give me my babe; I'll warm it at my breast.
Frank, take that toddling child. Walk all the rest—
    Pilgrims of Liberty.

Give our home to the flames, your portrait too,
I do not need that, love, while I have you;
    Yet it is dear to me.
Our children will be houseless now, poor things,
Yet they'll be blest, for happiness still flings
    Her blessings to the free.

We scorn to have them near a gilded chain,
Let them go barefoot if they may retain
    Sweet freedom at wealth's cost.
What though our eldest boys are half-clothed braves
(At any rate their children won't be slaves),
    More they fear shame than frost.

Say you it is too cold to take our babes
Out in the night air?   Husband, there are graves,
    Not in the old churchyard.
I'd rather leave my children in the snow
Than see them crouch to a despotic foe;
    Death, Liberty will guard.

You know that long I cannot bear the cold,
Too like a flower is what your arms enfold;
     So let us quickly go.
I'd teach my children how to suffer ere
A frosty plank will be my welcome bier,
     That he'll not want? the foe!

The dying blessing that my heart will crave,
My youngest girl to sleep within my grave;
     The rest I'll leave to you.
One can fight soon; and those who can't can pray;
I think God soon will hear what children say,
     And give our foe his due.

Not that! not that! I have no bitter hate
For the brave men who drive us from our gate;
     Pity, O Lord, such men;
Frank, teach our children not to hate, but fight,
And God after awhile will bless the right;
     They may come home again.

Let us go now—oh, how that north wind blows!
It seems to have the spirit of our foes.
     Thank God, that up in heaven
There'll be no envy, avarice, nor scorn,
Nor, worse, contempt for those who are forlorn,
     Nor Puritanic leaven.

Dared any think that we could traitors be?
We who were born free, false to liberty?
     What if Kentucky's sons
Have been betrayed? The noblest ever are
Easiest deceived. Now they spring to the war
     With rusty swords and guns.

Help me to wrap the children up, my love.
Why, Eddie must not cry! Now, if he'll prove
     Himself a 'little man,'
And will not fret when he is tired and cold,
I'll say my pet shall be a soldier bold;
     Is not that a fine plan?

Eight tender lambs to go into the snow !
O Savior ! who has trod the way of woe,
       Fold them upon Thy breast !
Or else, dear God, come down and for them fight ;
But let them die ere they forsake the right !
       When may the children rest ?

A traitorous mother's breast would feed a slave ;
God, let the unborn one rest in my grave.
       Oh, what unspoken bliss,
Never to know what means a tyrant's power !
But, thank God, child of ours will never cower
       At any power but His !

Husband, where is the match ?   We've stayed too
    long,
I hear the footsteps of an armed throng ;
       Thieves justified by law.
Step proudly, husband mine, you still are free,
Though we're bereft of all but liberty,
       By avarice's war.

A LITANY FOR 1861.

O God, our God, in this our hour of dark
And bitter dread, we flee to Thee.
       'Spare us,
Good Lord !' Oh, spread o'er us Thy shelt'ring wings,
And shield us from the pitiless and grim,
Barbaric foe !
       'Good Lord, deliver us '
From rapine and from blood.   Preserve to us
Our heritage of liberty, and let
Us not historic beacon be, to warn
All nations of the uselessness of law.
If our foes triumph, Lord, freedom must die.
O Father, God ! surely it cannot be

That Thou wilt give us up to eat 'the fruit
Of our own ways,' and perish in our pride.
Smite us—if it must be—but for awhile,
Only till we shall feel our need of Thee ;
Then raise us up again to liberty.
Give hearts of flesh to our relentless foe ;
Pity, dear God, his bigotry and scorn
Of mercy, law, of freedom and of truth.
'Graciously look on our afflictions, Lord ;
With pity see the sorrows of our hearts.'
Let us not ' fall into the hands of men '
Whom demons spirit on to work their will.
'O Lord, let Thy mercy be showed on us
As we do put our trust in Thee ! '   Amen.

A MODERN KNIGHT-ERRANT.

This morn a little blackamoor
   Brought me a funny thing, she said ;
And truly, on a stick she bore
   Something that many people dread.

Firm coat of mail of black and red,
   Well marked with rustic heraldry ;
A hidden or protruded head,
   And goose-like feet in mimicry.

Such was the quaint thing I perceived,
   And yet it pleased me very well,
For a long time have I believed
   Each breathing thing a tale may tell.

Therefore, I thought the terrapin
   Some curious lore might teach to me ;
So since the morning it hath been
   In my foot-tub for me to see.

The small thing, clad in mail unique,
   Looks quite strange in my china tub;
The queerness doth my fancy pique—
   Knight-errant I my turtle dub.

Don Quixotes are not yet extinct;
   We've Yankee ones enough, I trow;
Dutch Sanchos strut around, and wink
   To Sambos—their dear brothers now.

My turtle like such seems to be,
   Threatens my hand right off to snap;
A formidable knight is he,
   Some think so—till I give a slap

That rings upon his domicile;
   When straightway he doth hide his head
Beneath his shell, and lies quite still—
   The children have run off in dread.

Just so the Abolition fry
   Have snapped and snarled and raised a fuss.
Now to their homes they meekly hie,
   And ' wash their hands ' of all the ' muss.'

My turtle knight will eat no food,
   Thinking that he will thus spite me.
There is a philanthropic brood
   Will have no sugar in their tea.

Philanthropy will do quite well
   While it on the defensive acts,
But not when it would send to hell
   The masters—just to free the blacks.

Good people, let God rule His earth,
   He better comprehends, I trow,
The awful mysteries of birth ;
   Can't ye endure what He'll allow ?

True, ye are better than the saints
   Who ruled the Church in ancient days ;
No wonder the weak Christian faints
   When he your dread commands obeys.

But, thank God ! there is still a Church
   That has not snatched from Him the rod ;
Fanatics, would ye find her ?   Search
   For the old path Apostles trod.

My turtle thinks himself quite wise,
   And able to arrange my room ;
' The spider's fate is hard,' he cries,
   And then he snaps at Betsy's broom.

Sir turtle, if you'll quiet be,
   Some of the spiders yours shall be ;
He answers puritanicly,
   ' But they do not agree with me.'

As I can't eat them they must live,
   And have the freedom of your room ;
Pious is the advice I give.
   All day, like Yankee, doth he fume.

September 1861.

THE CLOUDS OF WAR.

The Washington *Star*, a semi-official of the Government, publishes the fact that the regular army officers are none of them Abolitionists.   Certainly not ; *they* all stay at home.

O God, the clouds of war press heavily !
I pant and pant ; now I can scarcely breathe,
I fear I cannot choose but suffer woe ;
No energy of hope have I to rise
Above the fog and darkness thick and strange :
Inhuman monsters loom through the gray mist,
Backed by the demons rising from below ;
They seem to cling fast to the forms I love.

My God, how can I breathe in such foul air?
I faint! I long to lay me down and sleep—
If I could sleep and dream of the old days
When peace and freedom dared to brave the light,
And man had naught to fear from brother man!
My heart is sick. My strength gives way. I lie
The abject slave of power and cruelty;
Not that my life hath felt the tyrant's lash
Of hate and jealousy, of wrong and fear,
But it is quite as bad to see it laid
Athwart the manhood of my Southern friends,
The hardest thought of all—the blows are dealt
By those I loved and honored, and once claimed
As brothers I prized most; for to the North
My heart had always clung admiringly.
Father, forgive! they know not what they do!

The lust of wealth has crazed humanity,
Brothers are brothers only when they ' pay;'
Ah! avarice doth wear the borrowed mask
Of patriotic zeal. O God, forgive
The old hypocrisy in its new guise.

I feel my palsied nerves are growing strong
As iron bands! let them not crush all life
From my awak'ning heart that hath so long
Been dead alike to any joy or grief,
For when I feel too much I know ere long
I shall feel none.
                     Father, is it that Thou
Dost numb the heart which Thou wilt sorely smite?
Well; be it as Thou wilt, I dare not choose
Aught for myself or those I dearest hold;
Except what I know always is Thy will—
Only, O God! prepare us for Thy home.
Then, though thick be the thorns that mark the way,
I will rejoice if it lead all to Thee.
    October 11.

YE SHALL BE FREE.

Ye *shall* be free,
For with our guns we will stand o'er you,
        Choke on our liberty
If so ye list; but what we say is true,
        Ye shall be free.

        Ye shall be free.
' All men are free, and equal born,' we say,
        Ye shall not greater be
Than we; or, die fit prey for liberty !
        Ye shall be free.

        Ye shall be free;
The right to rule ourselves reads but one way,
        That ye must will as we;
Govern yourselves ye may if as we say,
        Ye shall be free.

        Ye shall be free;
Napoleon, Europe forced to liberty,
        And we will do as he;
Nor he, nor we would hear of tyranny;
        Ye shall be free.

AROUSE, KENTUCKIANS.

Arouse, Kentuckians, or my heart will break !
What though by thousands brethren may forsake
Us in our bonds; if we are only strong,
Though but a remnant, we'll overcome the wrong
Which they and we have done our Mother State;
Arouse, Kentuckians, ere it be too late.

Come, fathers, to the fight, or ye will see
Your children groaning 'neath fierce slavery !
Richer are freemen poorly clothed and fed
Than millionaires who eat mute vassals' bread.
Haste, fathers ! leave your children to God's care ;
Those who are free much want and care can bear.

Come, husbands, if true women's love ye prize,
Can ye read their rebuke in mournful eyes ?
When other wives with joy and pride will flush,
Is it for you that yours will have to blush ?
Haste, husbands ! leave your dearest to God's care ;
While ye fight, victory they'll win by prayer.

Come, lovers ! shame on any one who lags
Behind his peers, while Lincoln freemen gags !
Your sweethearts' love will very soon grow cool,
Knowing ye are the butts for ridicule.
Haste, lovers, if true hearts ye would secure ;
The youth who holds back now must scorn endure.

Arouse, Kentuckians, now for love of fame !
Arouse, Kentuckians, now for fear of shame !
By all the pride we've had in our old State,
I charge ye, rescue her ere it is too late ;
Ye have no right to stain her glorious fame,
And leave the future a dishonored name.

Arouse, Kentuckians, now for love of those
Who have so nobly braved their Northern foes.
By old Virginia's desolated land,
I charge you, rise and join the courageous band
That battles for its liberties and rights,
The heaven-blessed heroes of a hundred fights.

Arouse, Kentuckians, by great Dan's praise,
We'll die ere we will desecrate the bays
With which he crowned us when he did confide
In old Kentucky. Ah ! no flag could hide
His mother's face ; he knew her by the heart
Which beat for him in spite of Yankee art.

L

Arouse, Kentuckians, by your love for those—
Your noblest sons—slain by their hireling foes!
Not even in your soil may they be laid
Who for your freedom with their life-blood paid.
Arouse, Kentuckians, now, or we are lost ;
Trust God, and stop not now to count the cost.

Arouse, Kentuckians, by the hateful sneer
Which Lincoln's despots give to soothe your fear :
Arouse ! avenge your wrongs upon the men
Who in the legislative halls again
Will dare to vote as ye have them forbid ;*
Rouse ye ! and of such Arnolds soon be rid.

Arouse, Kentuckians ! Each man to his gun !
Our struggle now in earnest has begun.
Your guns prepared, drill, and in quiet wait ;
Then when our army comes into the State,
We will be ready by its aid to gain
The freedom, else we'll sigh for but in vain.

Arouse, Kentuckians ! Shall bribed† papers' lies
Longer throw Yankee dust into your eyes ?
Teach all that ye will your own masters be—
That 'twas not fear which taught you slavery,
Only despair ; but now hope blooms for you,
Ye swear to freedom an allegiance true.

---

* Many members who were elected to defend the neutrality
of Kentucky, to refuse all aid to the U. S. Government by voting
either men or money, violated their pledges, avowed or admitted
when they were candidates. Of course, this stigma does not
rest upon all of the legislators ; some were arrested, some were
obliged to flee, and a minority of those who were left stood up
nobly for the principles to which they were committed.

† It is laughable to see the sudden 'wheel-about' of the
Louisville papers.

A PATRIOT'S DEATH THE SIGN OF A BRIGHTER MORROW.

'A red sunset is indicative of a fair morrow.'

Air—' Tom Moore.'

In blood the sun is setting,
  That this morn arose in clouds;
How many warriors are sleeping
  To-night in their battle-shrouds !

But the clouds that in the morn
  Were heavy and cold and gray,
A free Southern breeze has fast driven
  Afar to the North away.

Alas ! that in blood must set
  A spirit of breath Divine;
But the Christian hero to-morrow
  In a brighter heaven will shine.

His death on a blood-red field
  Is promise of brighter days;
And the weary, lone watcher at home
  In a hopeful spirit prays.

THE TWELFTH STAR.

Kentucky seceded in convention assembled at Mayfield.

Kentucky's the twelfth Star. Now she is great,
Greatest in her forgetfulness of self;
Little have we to make by union with
The South—but what of that ? We do not live
For money but for love and righteousness,
For Christian brotherhood and sympathy.

L 2

My State, I glow in your manliness;
I knew that when your eyes, the spell o'ercome,
Were open to behold the ' cloven foot '
Of Northern Mammon, and the hidden sword
Of its proud twin, deceitful Tyranny,
With the Confederacy you would join.
A golden bait was thrown : you might have sold
Your slaves, and been the humored child
Of fond and foolish North, weak pet, and last
Of Imbecility, fit type of greed
And tyranny ; but better fate is yours.

October 1861.

AFRAID OF A DEAD BABY.

Mrs. S. B. Buckner asked, and was refused, permission to bring her child's corpse to Louisville for interment. She was at the time in Bowling Green with her husband.

Keep here, my little baby : rest alone !
    Not in thy fathers' tomb can'st thou be laid ;
And a brave warrior's wife must give no groan,
    Nor mother's grief the father's cause upbraid ;
For, thinks a savage enemy, my babe,
    A parent's heart breaking o'er youngest dead,
Is a fit object to make men afraid ;
    A weeping mother a fit spy to dread !

Surely, my boy, that naught but fear most rare
    Could make inhuman monsters of armed men,
That they'd refuse to let a mother bear
    A lifeless body to its home again ;
Thy father's soul can never understand
    The littleness of such tyrannic fear ;
E'en a false legislator* of the land
    Might be permitted freely to come here.

* Judge Underwood, to whom Gen. Buckner gave permission to enter and leave his lines at pleasure.' He, like many other

Brave hearts, like his, do not fear even men;
  What shall I call those who fear a dead babe?
Keep here, my boy, a little while, and when
  Thy birthplace is redeemed thou'lt find a grave.

THE BROTHERLY KINDNESS OF 1861.

'They' would burst Southern hearts in twain,
Nor care if so they could regain
The power and wealth that they have lost,
Aye, wealth at thousands of souls' cost!
God save us from the tender love
That lean hawk has for well-fed dove!
God save us from the love absurd
That from the cannon's mouth is heard!
Which proves its truth by fire and shell,
And sending brothers' souls to hell;
Loathsome is their hypocrisy,
Far worse than their cupidity.
To prove their love they put our men
On straw beds in a crowded den—
The stone floors emblems of the hearts
That dare not speak aloud their thoughts
Which we can by their deeds explain.
They're fighting only to regain
Advantages that they have lost,
To be paid for at freedom's cost.
So their forefathers gained much fame
By self-will in religion's name.
Pilgrims for conscience' sake they called
Themselves, whom jealousy had galled

legislators, sanctioned acts his State had denounced. Gen. B.'s
letter to Judge U. is as noble as possible; I am told a lady said
it turned her heart to the South.

Into a well-concerted plan
To independent be of man.*
But all who came to the New World
Must follow them, or soon be hurled
In prison, or submit to fine,
Or loss of limb, till they'd resign
Such an absurd thing as a will:
Bishop's chair did twelve bigots fill,†
And as they were low parvenus,
You must expect that they'd abuse
Their power, and lord it with grand air
O'er men and women when they dare.
Their spirit lives in the North now,
Their children Union now avow
To be the dearest thing in life,
Worth any new amount of strife.

SHOT!

O Brain, come quickly with your art!
Show me some scenes to calm my heart;
If you can't views of meeting bring,
Some poems of his bright youth sing.
But base Camp Douglas‡ keep afar!
And to Blue-Coats my vision bar.

---

* No one thoroughly educated in history needs be told that
the Puritan Fathers sailed from Calvinistic Holland, where they
had lived eleven or twelve years; and that they were months
negotiating for a commercial charter, and avowed that they
crossed the ocean to make money. As for freedom of conscience,
they never even thought of such a thing, but defended persecution
on principle.

† The great Milton is responsible for this.

‡ Camp Douglas has the worst reputation of any prison in
the United States. Prisoners of war are there tortured. A
writer in a loyal paper gives more than one instance of this.—ED.

For oh ! I don't want to go mad
By thinking of the woes he had
For freedom's sake to undergo.
But, God, I *will* not hate his foe ;
I will not think of what one did
Who threw a pall of death amid
All phantoms of my day or night.
From under it I grope for light,
To guide my heart where it may see
How my woe his great joy may be ;
And patiently while I live here
I'll quietly sit by his bier.
If he is happy in God's smile,
Where sin and war cannot defile,
My blessed child ! my only one !
What matter if there is no sun
To cheer the race my feet must run,
If at the last I'm only meet
To sit with my child at Christ's feet ?

THE CAPTURED FLAG.

'Gen. Buell has very kindly permitted us to exhibit the
secession flag taken by Gen. Thomas from the rebel forces of
Zollicoffer. It is in our office, where those anxious to see the
trophy can be gratified.'—*Louisville Journal.*

It is not strange that you should like to get
  Sight of the flag that waved
O'er Bull Run, Manassas, Somerset,
  And elsewhere, when you've craved

The quarter that you would not grant to those
  Who, scattered, dare to think
Of what the Constitution says ; such foes
  You in a dungeon sink.

Oh, despots ! fit it is you should rejoice
  O'er Zollicoffer dead ;
For, ever hath he raised a noble voice—
  Such as the tyrants dread.

God grant that we who fight for liberty
    May never thrust our hands
Into the manacles as willingly
    As they of Northern lands.

The rights for which we fight and dare to die
    Our children must hold fast,
Nor e'er to conquer one another try,
    Lest liberty, aghast,

Should, shrieking, flee from South as now from North
    She flees.   Unconscious they,
Who for our treasures seek, that hidden moth
    Eateth their own away.

Gaze on our captured flag; boast while you may;
    It's the first chance you've had.
Look at it now; perchance that the next day
    You see it you'll be sad.

How often have earth's despots gathered round
    The corpse of liberty,
And kept a lawless wake that they had ground
    To death those who were free!

But suddenly a stirring in the air*
    Hath made the tyrants' hearts
Beat rapidly.   What if the corpse should dare
    To rise and aim new darts?

Glory not much that you have gained one fight,
    You, who are used to run:
Our hearts are strong, for God is with the right;
    We wait the morrow's sun.

January 29, 1862.

           * Rev. ii. 8-11.

AWAY WITH THE STRIPES.

Ho! away with the stripes—the despot's fit flag!
The stars and the stripes are the bully's great
    'brag;'
The men who are bravest scorn falsehood and boasts:
No more shall the braggarts' flag marshal our hosts.

Chorus.

    Lord of the Cross,* our banner bless!
    O'erthrow the foe who would oppress
    And strangle liberty.
    God grant us victory!

Ho! away with the stripes! oh, carry them forth;
If ye leave them here they'll be food for the moth;
For liberty's sons the last time have unfurled
The flag that proclaims lawlessness to the world.
             Chorus.—Lord of the Cross, &c.

For scorn of a free press, of freedom of speech,
Of Habeas Corpus, is what the stripes teach;
Fallen stars gem the crown of Uncle Sam's king,
So with wholesome disgust drop we the foul thing.
             Chorus.—Lord of the Cross, &c.

Our foes say they're loyal—yes, Seward's their king;
True, Lincoln would be, but he cannot—poor
    thing!
The Democrats yet have some will of their own;
Who knows but that we may save them from a
    throne?
             Chorus.—Lord of the Cross, &c.

Ha! is it not funny that Yankees declare
The Union's too precious for the bold South to dare

* The battle-flag of the C. S. A. is a blue cross on a red field.

To draw back from the compact that *they*'ve broken
first?
But what they call 'treason' is lessening their
purse.

Chorus.—Lord of the Cross, &c.

The old Constitution they trampled in dust;
We've changed it a little—who best kept the
trust?
Ho! come, noble men, to be free let us dare,
The Cross of the South consecrates Southern air.

Chorus.—Lord of the Cross, &c.

Then, rally, ye freemen! be gentle as brave,
Be sons of the Cross that doth over you wave;
Spare an enemy vanquished, aye, pity the foe,
And the Lord of the Cross before you will go.

Chorus.—Lord of the Cross, &c.

If we would prove worthy of liberty's smile
No scorn of a brother our hearts must defile;
The poor man shall have equal rights with the rich,
But can't make a law to throw gold in a ditch.

Chorus.—Lord of the Cross, &c.

Northern mills shan't control the growth of our
lands,
But free shall it go where'er commerce demands.
Fanatics won't own us as Christians and men—
The fanatics cut loose, where will they drift then?

Chorus.—Lord of the Cross, &c.

The same symbol we bear aloft in the air,
Is worn over hearts that beat for us in prayer;
Whene'er we behold it our hands will defend
The helpless and prayerful, for God is their friend.

Chorus.

Lord of the Cross, our banner bless!
O'erthrow the foe who would oppress
And strangle liberty.
God grant us victory!

A NORTHERN MOTHER AFTER A BATTLE.

Throb, my heart, throb! for thy dear country throb!
There's nothing else left thee, for Death did rob
    Thee of thy joy.
But that's no reason why thou should'st not beat
With joy for victory, mourn for defeat.
    True, the dear boy
Can't to thy greetings, which were once too fond,
From out his bloody grave laugh or respond—
    But what of that?
Both North and South, men knew that Death would
    be
The conqueror of both the slave and free.
    Hell's concordat
Of war and rapine they did gladly sign,
And only one of many hearts is mine,
    That they have broke.
But I know I have no right to complain;
Some men great fortunes make and some fame gain.
    What though fields soak
In bright red blood, and laugh in sparkling gore!
It matters not. A few'll win fame, and more
    Will fortunes make;
And as for broken hearts—tut! what are they?
Only balls with which politicians play
    For their own sake.

THE OLD NEGRO AT CALHOUN'S GRAVE.

I saw in one of our daily papers a letter from some Northerner,
stating that an old negro put fresh flowers every morning on
Calhoun's grave. The letter was written about the time the
orange is in blossom.

Who comes with tottering step and slow,
Bowed not so much by years as woe,
Through old St. Philip's churchyard gate?
Whose love can twelve years not abate?

Strange that an old man bears fresh flowers !
The gray head comes from orange-bowers,
And lays love's tribute, sweet and fair,
On Calhoun's grave—his daily care.

' Master was always good to me,'
Says the poor slave we came to free.
And we reply, that ' Whence we came
Are some who curse your master's name.'

' They never knew him, then,' he said ;
' Why, he gave us our daily bread,
And everything we had beside :
Would he had lived and I had died ! '

' Old man, we've come to set you free ; '
' Oh, no ! I'll never go with ye ;
Ye told me that some cursed *his* name
In the bad land from whence ye came.'

' Your present master'll soon be poor ; '
' He'll never drive me from his door.'
' He'll not have for himself a crust ; '
' I don't know that ; in God we trust.'

' Those flowers we'd like to buy and save '—
' What ! sell flowers from old Massa's grave !
Now, go away and let me pray,
For wicked thoughts I've had to-day.'

FORT DONELSON FALLS.

Written in great agony, 3 P.M., February 17.

Demons, hark ! those cannons booming ;
  Death howls over liberty,
Which the despots are entombing !
  Let us die or still be free !

Ah! had I been of that true band
   That, my country, died for thee,
Joyfully had I grasped death's hand,
   Knowing I'd wed liberty.

Thou bravest, gentlest, noblest man,
   Would that I had man been born;
Then while thy life-blood o'er me ran,
   Sweetly had I smiled in scorn.

For the oppressor cannot go
   O'er ' the river, dark ' and deep;
There, safe from the insulting foe,
   Edward, with thee I would sleep!

God, our God, art gone for ever?
   Left us in our Southern pride?
Now from life our bodies sever;
   Let them die—our hearts have died.

Give the torches to the women,
   Children will the matches hold;
Free let us live in swamp and fen,
   Wives and sisters of the bold!

Blessed those who died in armor!
   Let us shed no tears for them;
Thrice-blessèd eyes that never saw
   Avarice wear the diadem!

But we weep for the true-hearted,
   Quiet martyrs of the strife,
Who from their brave brothers parted,
   To guard mother, child, or wife.

Such I know, a son of duty;
   His is more than martyr's woe;
Must his feelings be the booty
   Of the vain, exultant foe?

Yet forgive we, Savior, like Thee,
  Those who their foul hands imbue
In life-blood of our liberty,
  For 'they know not what they do.'

LAST NIGHT AT FORT DONELSON.

Inscribed to Col. Charles Johnson, of Gen. Buckner's Staff.

Night falleth, grim, on the exhausted men
Who've won three battles in four days:
Pounceth the crowding foe on strengthless men,
For even now they scarce can walk or stand:
God pity the brave but exhausted band!
Let us fight but one hour and we are tired,
Four days they've fought—Sampson's to be admired
By all who honor fearlessness and skill!
Ah, if they had but as much strength as will!
Then never would the noble Spartan band
Yield e'en one inch of their loved Southern land.
Spartan I called it; yes, but Christian too.
They have done all that valiant men can do.
Although but one to six, they've kept at bay
Fresh Western men four days—done what *men* may.

Now, shall they die like heathens every one,
And let us say their deaths have nothing done?
For sure if this exhausted band were dead,
The land would still quake beneath foreign tread.
What more can they do that they have not done?
Buckner and his brave men have victory won.
Success is not mere tangible effect—
Valor has triumphed, though the fort's a wreck.
If one man can keep six in check four days,
When we fight 'one to three' we'll win the bays;
This is the problem solved at Donelson,
And they who proved it a great victory won.

Nor cold, nor heat, nor hunger, nor death-pains
Can conquer hearts where love of country reigns.
Sleepless and shelterless, four days and nights,
With wounds and frosted feet, our army fights.
Seldom has history to memory given
Longer-lived valor, when the soul has striven
For love of liberty, the flesh to nerve
With superhuman power, that it might serve
To be like rock in path of avalanche,
If it might but retard the foe's advance.
There is no fire in these men's sunken eyes,
Nor more than stripling's strength in their war-cries;
When they receive a wound they only creep
Aside that they may have a chance to sleep.
One fires and kills his foe, then shuts his eyes;
One stands and sleeps while his companion dies;
It's not mere flesh and blood that thus can fight—
Oh, no ! for to my sympathetic sight
There is revealed a cordon of brave hearts,
And ever through the chain one word fast darts
Electric, binding all in unity
Of firm resolve—that word is Liberty.

But now, as of old time, it is decreed
That ere it can be won true hearts must bleed ;
And some must pass their days while laws decay,
From cause they love, in dungeon chill and gray.
Alike are such a needed sacrifice,
And with the victors will receive fame's prize ;
Their country only asks that they will do
What may be done by spirits brave and true,
Forbids them e'er to throw their lives away,
That they may fight for her rights another day.

Shall Buckner sacrifice eight thousand lives,
For fear mean-minded men will *him* despise ?
Go, ask the wives whose husbands in the fights
Have rested not four weary days and nights,

If those they love Buckner shall sacrifice ?
Are God-bought souls *his* vain, ambitious prize ?
What *right* has he to sacrifice the men,
Whom he might send to frantic hearts again ?
' These are his men,' Satan suggests ; ' they came
Up to the fort to fight and die for fame.'

Not so, O Tempter ! self is not the god
Of patriots—if so they need the rod
Of their land's fiercest scorn.   Our Washington
Retreated when he could not win ; does shame
Attach itself to his most honored name ?
There was in Eastern lands a pyramid
Formed of a thousand skulls ; the builder bid
It stand for ever, monument of fame.
Dare *Christians* say they'd like to see the same
Reared on our Southern land to Buckner's name ?
' Buckner should have retreated,' some cry out ;
Yes, he could have escaped, without a doubt,
If self had been the monarch of the hour ;
He, *like himself*, prepared to guard the flower
Of chivalry in this its trying hour ;
All can't escape, who'll be the sacrifice ?
Those who have won from selfish fame the prize.

March 8.

ONE CAUSE OF THE WAR.

The man who trusts not God betrays himself,
Weak victim he to that foul harpy, wealth ;
Let him bid farewell to joy, peace and health.

A slave henceforth of most tormenting cares,
Boldly proclaiming what no devil dares,
That man no part of God's provision shares.

And so one said ere he'd foreseen this war,
' I have my fortune now to make or mar,
And to my will there is no let nor bar.'

War God has sent to punish such as he,
Who scorn His hand in anything to see,
And think as they declare the world must be.

ON ASH-WEDNESDAY, 1862.

The six weeks' Sabbath has begun ;
A little while, my soul, be done
With heat and flurry of life's race ;
Take time to cultivate God's grace.

Most of the seeds He sowed are lost,
Those that are left are passion-tost :
Save them, heart, ere it be too late ;
Redeem them from pride, scorn, and hate.

Think less now of thy country's rights,
And rise above the jeers and slights
Of those who know no Lenten fast ;
Thy last sneer, let it be thy last.

Thy country asketh much of thee ;
Do all, but let thy motto be,
If we will make God's law our care,
Our country 'neath His wings He'll bear.

Work for the Southern sick and poor,
The prayer for prisoners read o'er ;
Prize as thou wilt each Southern arm
That strikes to shield thee from alarm.

But scorn not him who hates us most,
Pity thy foes' malicious boast ;
' In quietness shall be thy strength ; '
Thy Savior will awake at length.

M

Our faith to try, He seems to sleep.
Think of the past and do not weep;
He will arise when we have learned
To honor Him who vainly yearned

A long while since to shield from harm
Those who refused His sheltering arm.
When we have found we cannot walk
Without protector in the dark,

He will arise and set us free :
Art *ready*, heart, for liberty ?
Can'st rise superior to thy foe,
By ne'er exulting o'er his woe ?

Can'st conquer pride of vanquished men
By never showing pride again ?
Art ready to forgive all wrong ?
Can God now trust thee to be strong ?

But while the victory doth delay,
Be patient, heart, and learn to pray,
That when victorious days may dawn,
We'll know no hate, revenge, or scorn.

This for thy country ; but for thee,
O heart, pray thou may'st now be free ;
Loosened from chains of self and will,
Content to bear whatever ill

Thy Father knows is best for thee :
Trust Him, for farther He can see
Than thou. Think of thy love-marked past—
Easter comes after Lenten fast.

For one, who in thy cradle lay,
With fasting and great fervor pray
That God may save his precious life
In the mad hours of fiery strife.

Six others with blood of my race
Are ready the fierce foe to face;
Friends and acquaintances by scores
Now front the avalanche, which pours

From Northern lands, to overwhelm
The 'sunny South.'   The joyous realm
Of flowers and birds and happy hearts!
Happy, I mean, before the darts

Of jealousy pierced Northern brains:
O God! remember all our pains!
Hush, heart! Lent is the time to think
How many souls are on the brink

Of endless bliss or misery.
How many will owe life to thee?
Thy Lent-work speedily begin,
To conquer thine and others' sin.

'BOY WHO THINKEST TO BE WED.'

Boy who thinkest to be wed,
By remembrance of our dead,
Rest not till the foe be fled.

Thy unburied brother lies
On battle-field; his glazed eyes
Stare in sorrow's mute surprise

That he is forgot so soon,
While thou talk'st of honeymoon.
But he will not ask a boon

Of a soul as base as thine;
Else he'd ask thee to decline
Love and joy, and to combine

With men to win him the right*
To lie where he first saw light;
But, slave, thou'rt afraid to fight!

Dance, boy, gaily with thy bride!
Thou hast not man's heart or pride;
Would thou wert by brother's side!

Then we would not blush for thee,
For we would know thou art free.
Now, boy, run thy bride to see!

VIOLETS IN LENT.

Light is breaking from the clouds,
Wintry snow no more enshrouds
Violets which bloom in crowds.

Bees are humming in the air,
And their dusky wings seem fair,
Seen when bright spring days are rare.

God we feel is overhead,
And His wings about us spread
Melteth now the frozen dread.

Which none lets another know,
Of our most rapacious foe.
God now mitigates that woe

With a hope that when it's warm,
Brothers and our friends will swarm
Round us to shield us from harm.

* It is against the law for relations to bring into Kentucky,
for burial, Confederate soldiers; and some have been denied the
privilege of moving their dead from one part of Kentucky to
another.—ED.

Father, chant I now Te Deum ;
Feeling that ere long they'll come,
My heart beats like the bees' hum.

Prophesy that summer's near,
Though now but few flowers appear ;
God of flowers, our Lent prayers hear !

LINCOLN'S ROYAL RECEPTION.

First Cæsar came, and bent the knee to one
Who reigns in Washington :—
' The Brutus of my day is dead in yours, therefore
Your subjects will bear more
Than mine of eighteen hundred years ago.
Down with the eagle ! perch the crow
Above the banners of your minions base ;
Bid them feast on the dead
And mangled form of haughty liberty,
Whose ghost upbraided me ;
But now I think she will for ever sleep,
For prostrate thousands creep
At your command, to make on earth their hell.
Great Lincoln, fare you well ! '

Then came a baffled man, the tyrant John,
Pilgrim to Washington :—
' All hail ! O greatest of all despots, hail !
Before you I must quail ;
I tried to overawe a people rude,
Whose thoughts, unlearned and crude,
Made me acknowledge myself but a fool ;
But you are no such tool
To tyrant law and unlearned statesmanship.
Here, Lincoln, is the whip
I tried upon the backs of restive men,
Who " laid " it on me then ;

Ill-mannered churls !   Your subjects, more polite,
Will never thus requite
Your efforts to rule o'er them for your good ;
Would I in your place stood ! '

Then came Napoleon :—' Lincoln, you are great,
Superior to your fate,
Though I succumbed to mine, and died remote
From those I loved and smote ;
But over those you hate you rule secure,
In despotism pure.
I tried to palliate my harsh decrees ;
But you do as you please,
Nor even try to sugar-coat the pill—
Whole-swallowed at your will.
I rested peacefully within my tomb
Until fate spoke my doom :
" Napoleon, you are very small indeed
Henceforth in tyrants' creed ;
Lincoln is now the first, the second you."
I know these words are true,
So place my iron crown upon your head,
And, howling, seek the dead.'

Then entered one, with long and solemn face,
Said a New England grace,
And thus began : ' First of fanatics, eat !
With swift peace-sandalled feet
I've hastened, luscious food to bring to you ;
Here's a dish that's quite new.'
' Faugh ! Butternuts ! ' said Lincoln, and grew sick ;
But he revived right quick
When he perceived that they were nicely cracked.
He tasted them and smacked
His lips, and cried, ' O Cromwell, king of saints !
You've cured all my complaints :
These nuts are good, with blood of hearts prepared.
The fools their heads have bared ;

I've but to say the word, and they'll succumb.
I know it. They were dumb
While Hill and I had in the South grand times;
They who endorsed those crimes
Have proved themselves too weak, dread to inspire—
House-burned they'll call out "Fire!"'
'Beware,' said Noll; 'first play a little joke
On the great men who croak;
And then you are secure to work your will.
A few men you must kill—
May, Cox, and Pendleton, Powell, Voorhees—
Then do just as you please.'

[There are a few other members of Congress worthy of
Lincoln's revenge, but metre forbade my naming all.]

A RUMOUR OF PEACE.

I think a voice divine hath stirred the air;
  I do not breathe so heavily.
Without, for winter, it is wondrous fair:
  A bird sings on that leafless tree.

Oh, say again that there are hopes of peace!
  With blessed words sweet silence break.
Can it be that barbarity will cease
  Echoes in ruined lives to wake?

O Lord! in the Bethesda porch we wait,
  A crowd of woe, poor, sick, and lame;
Let angel cast in bloody pool base hate
  And savage strife—a 'fig' for fame!

Let our beloved ones come into our arms—
  We ask no spoils of victory;
Dearer to us than military charms,
  The graces of humanity.

Yet much, O God ! we thank Thee who hast blest
    The Southern arms with victory ;
Upon our knees, hands clasped in thankful rest,
    We offer praise for liberty.

A RICHMOND HEROINE.

Air—‘ Lass o’ Gowrie.’

‘ A daughter of the proprietor of the Tredegar Iron Works at
Richmond was captured by our advancing forces last week,
beyond Great Bethel, in the act of signalling our approach to
the enemy. She braved all the consequences of her acts, and is
now in Fort McHenry paying the penalty of her feminine rashness, but is not in the least abashed by her conduct ; on the
contrary, she manifests all the usual symptoms of the rebel
disease. She is a pretty girl of some eighteen or nineteen
summers.’—*New York Post.*

A pretty girl, through whose soft hair
Daintily played warm Southern air,
Quickly threw up a round white arm.
Grave was she, for she gave alarm,
To those who battle for their land,
That foreign foe was close at hand.

I think as her arm bravely went
Up with the signal, valor lent
Its vigor to her maiden heart,
And bade her act the patriot’s part,
As surely as it nerves the man
Who leads the stalwart battle-van.

She knew that she might have to lie
In dungeon, or might have to die ;
The foe fears Southern women fair,
And well he may, for much we’d dare,
But the brave daughters of our land
Fear not to fall by tyrant’s hand ;

Better to die by coward's blow,
Than smile above our country's woe!
So thinks the heroine who dwells
In prison now; but her heart swells,
And rises on triumphant wings
Over barred gates, and downward flings,
Into each Southern sister's heart,
The wish to emulate her part.
It is not that we crave her fame
That in her place we'd do the same;
Share with the men the patriot's meed,
And dare to act upon the creed
Learned from the life of Washington—
Freedom is worthy to be won.

THE CHURCH OF THE SOUTH TO THE CHURCH OF THE NORTH.

Written on reading an article in the *Church Journal* of New York, which I cannot now find.

We are not divided—no, never! no! no!
For the Church of the North cannot be our foe;
Our hearts fill with reverence, with love and trust,
For mother whose robes are not tainted with dust
Of politics' labyrinths; pure is the hem
Of your garments, and so our love's diadem
(For we honor the Church that scorns a base end).
We lie down at your feet, our mother, our friend.
Our friend—yes, when we had none other save God.
We will not forget this when you feel the rod;
For fanatics may soon wave over you, too,
The sword which at first for our bosoms they drew.

By your compass we'll steer if our bark, storm-tost,
Fanatics and demagogues fain would cry 'Lost;'
Then, mother, we'll try to prove worthy of you,
Nor the Church's pure hands in man's blood imbrue.

Though we differ as men, to God we'll be true,
And to bow to State-craft will refuse, we as you ;
Nor let money-changers, pretending to serve
The Church and her Master, e'er cause us to swerve
From prayer and from praise, from peace and good-will,
Lest Christ should scourge us as promoters of ill.

O mother, much-honored, if all could but know
That if any earth-power could e'er cause to grow
Together again the members now severed,
It would be the Church.*   She only endeavoured
To heel bleeding hearts, bind up festering sores :
If Church had ruled State we might still be indoors.
But now we go forth in a pitiless world.
Yet one tie still binds us.   See what is unfurled
Above our true hearts ; though passion's begun
To draw us apart, on our banner is ' one.'
But 'tis one with our mother in doctrine and faith,
And next to God's word we'll honor, ' she saith.'
Two nations are we, but one Church for ever—
Fanatics His bride from Christ cannot sever.
We know that in State we could never agree,
As men you are ' loyal,' and democrats we ;
But not against you do our hearts now rebel,
Not for popular praise Christ's Church did you sell.†
We've naught to complain of,‡ you did not forget,
That ' terms of communion ' by a Master were set ;
Who said of His kingdom, ' it is not of earth,'
For this may He save you from sorrow and dearth.

* Benton, in *Thirty Years in the United States' Senate*, records
the verdict of Calhoun, that the Episcopal Church was the only
one that could maintain the Union.

† Since this was written there has been a general convention
in New York city, and cries of disloyal men heard even in the
church where it sat, as the populace hooted outside.

‡ When the Southern Church found it necessary to separate
its ecclesiastical jurisdiction from that of the Northern, it said it
had no cause of complaint against Churchmen of the North who
had never insulted them.

Although we are grown, and as men we must roam,
Your arms open, mother, and let us go home
On some blessed festival, kneel by your side,
And praise our good God that you have not defied
The rules He has given to govern His bride ;
We'll come to you, mother, forgetful of pride
That fences the South as with cordons of steel ;
Not as men do we blush ; as Christians we feel.

If e'er the time comes that you need our strong-arm,
We'll lay down our lives to defend you from harm ;
The heart of the South may be proud, but it's true,
And still it beats warmly, sweet mother, for you.

The soldiers we shrink from on week-days as foes,
When we see in our churches, we hush to repose
The feelings of earth, for one Father is ours,
Nor step-brethren we ; our mother's form towers
Above that of the North.   Our Southern hearts pray
That we and that they may our parents obey.
Whene'er child of yours near us suffering lies,
We'll think of our mother and drown party cries ;
And when the war's over some brethren there'll be—
No.—While we can *honor*, your children are we.*

TO MADAME THERESE PULSZKY,

Who, with her husband, followed Gen. Kossuth in his exile.

I'm gazing on the pleasant face,
    And thinking of the time
    When in our Western clime
Thou gav'st to me memento fair, to grace

* The writer of this hopes most earnestly that the next
general convention will try to establish a general council, to
which the Churches of the Confederacy, the United States,
England, Sweden, Moravia, &c., might be invited.

My room of books; I took it from thy hand
   With a sweet girlish thrill.
   'Twas not that thou could'st trill
Wild Eastern lays to our young western land

That gave thee deepest interest for me;
   But that thou wast exiled,
   From lands despots defiled,
And that thyself could'st a companion be

Of one who for great freedom boldly struck,
   Was baffled, had to roam;
   'Twas well to leave his home
To tyrants' pigs, that fatten on the muck

Of the untended flowers and rotten fruits
   Which beautified the spot
   Where liberty was not
Allowed to dwell.   Leave it to whom it suits.

I pitied thee, but thought not I could be
   Ever exposed to fate
   Like thine; yet it may wait
For me.   Like thee, I'll bear it cheerfully,

And let to all my simple presence say,
   Behold! I am not sad,
   For freedom can make glad
One who no other cause has to be gay.

If we could meet now I would say to thee,
   Worthy am I to be
   Sister in liberty;
For I, too, scorn a home where I'm not free.

And I am like to thee in one thing more;
   We both await the hour
   Of bloom for freedom's flower,
And feel it yet will blossom by our door.

THE UNITED STATES' EAGLE.

' Straws show the way that the wind blows ; '
And I've often thought an emblem grows
Out of the thing it represents
As naturally as the rents
Of smoke show where the fire's concealed,
Or scar tells of a wound that's healed.

The eagle is of birds the king,
That is, the most rapacious thing ;
It uses its great breadth of wing
Itself upon a lamb to fling.

Can anything dare say to it,
' I think I have a right to sit
Out in the sun—enjoy myself ? '
' Not so ! you're made for eagle's health.
What would preserve his stomach's tone
If you were to be "let alone ? " '

The eagles dwell in Northern land ;
Yankees and eagles—whew ! how grand !
'Tis true the mocking bird prefers
To stay away from Northern curs,
But if the eagle thinks it's best
That barking should disturb its rest,
The mocking-bird had better learn
No more for quietness to yearn.

I am too fast ; for I have heard
That e'en the very smallest bird
Sometimes picks out the eyes of great
And pompous ones.   It is too late
When eagle cannot see to roam,
To wish that he had stayed at home.
How sweet to think that there may be
Again a time when the South, free

From the coarse scream of Northern bird,
Its mocking songster may be heard.
When war has left a doom of night
For those whose dearest died in fight,
The Southern bird will lift the gloom
That hangeth over free men's tomb,
And carol in the mourner's ear
Such notes as cannot fail to cheer;
Then darkness will grow clear and warm,
And consecrate to many a form
That gave its life on land or sea,
Glad sacrifice for Liberty.

And so the night will pass away
In calm content, the while we pray,
Nor will a Tory heart regret
That no more can the eagle fret
The Southern bird with threat to seize
Its nest and eggs whene'er it please.

O eagle! just 'let us alone!'
For we want nothing but our own;
Our belles will gladly wear homespun
If rid of Vandal and of Hun,
Children be pleased with fewer toys
To get rid of the Yankee boys
Who come to fight and stay to steal.
Not in our day can the wound heal,
Which avarice and love of power
Inflicted in Satanic hour
Upon our justice-loving land.
O Yankee, go!   We'll give our hand
At parting; if you will but go,
We'll pardon you our heaped-up woe.
Ah! we have learned in a 'dear school,'
That he who trusts to man's a fool;
The right to rule ourselves we hold—
Sir Yankee, you are over-bold.

April 29.

'PARDON AND PEACE.'

'Pardon and peace!' what music in those words,
    Meet for the angels' song!
But needed more by men—the sinful herds
    Who now hell's pathway throng.
The voice of mercy's drowned by cries of war,
    E'en woman's heart's oft hushed
To pity's groan; and justice lags afar,
    And piety is crushed
Under the iron heels of Satan's scouts,
    Who rush before the car,
Where sits the Yankee Juggernaut. Flee, doubts,
    Which treacherously bar
With faithlessness God's entrance to our aid.
    Friends, 'put on charity!'
'Be pitiful!' forgive those who have made
    Your peace—in trembling flee
Your land as burial-grounds, where ye may see
    The stones that mark the graves
Where sleep your laws and liberty.
    Let not your hearts be slaves
To vengeance, or to enmity;
    But trust to Him who saves.

TO COLONEL JOHN H. MORGAN,
2nd Regiment Kentucky Cavalry.

Our hero-chief, Kentucky's pride,
To whom she gladly doth confide
Her chivalry, renowned of yore!
A braver man her name ne'er bore.
Kentucky vaunts thy chivalry;
But prouder still is she to see
That in the days when women are
Oft boasted captives of the war,

Her nobler sons have not forgot
The courtesy that doth allot
To them the freedom of the weak—
Not such the victims brave men seek.

But here, where Northmen are around,
It is a most refreshing sound
To hear that to a woman's prayer
Her husband was released.   Oh ! rare
Such chivalry to us doth seem !
And, Morgan, thou would'st think I dream
If I'd tell how from morn till night
Yankees and Prentice talk and write
Of how the women shall be ' paid '
For giving sympathy and aid
To *wounded captives* ; thus with shame
The Yankees brand Kentucky's name.

O Morgan, come ! we long for thee ;
Then women may again be free.
Let this be first of your decrees—
' O Yankee fair, do what you please,
For we are not afraid of men,
How can we be of women, then ? '
The Yankee women can't despise
The man who all the earth defies
To find one braver in a fight,
More valiant for what is right,
Or gentler to the captive foe,
More pitiful to human woe.

Kentucky women call for thee
To come and give them liberty.
Thou never turnest a deaf ear
To those who cry from grief or fear
That thou wilt come to their relief.
Now rescue *us*, our Hero-Chief !

A PRAYER FOR THE SOUTH.

O God! my heart goes up to Thee
For our brave men on land and sea,
Who fight the battles of the free;
    God grant them victory!

They are our noblest and our best,
Who bravely bear the freeman's crest,
And march at Liberty's behest;
    Father, may they be blest!

The mother's pride, her only boy,
The maiden's life, her only joy,
Have gone forth that they may decoy
    The eagle, and destroy.

For it has perched itself above
The nest of free-born Southern dove—
Intruder no true heart can love;
    God save the poor, wronged dove!

The banner that we used to prize
Has been defiled before our eyes,
And in dishonored tatters lies
    On soil that our blood dyes.

We only want what is our own,
That we are free we long have known,
Nor will we other master own
    Than Him on heaven's throne.

We know that we have done amiss;
But any punishment than this—
That worse men may in hate's abyss
    Destroy our envied bliss!

The chastisement we must receive
We'll take as from Thy hands; reprieve
Us soon, O Lord!   Our prayers receive —
    Oh, pity and relieve!

N

THE BRIDAL GIFT.

' Fair one, soon my bride to be,
What shall be my gift to thee ? '
' Wilt thou give me what I ask ?
If so, I'll set thee a task.'
' Which I will most gladly do
With rewarding smiles in view.'
' For bridal gift I'll freedom take ;
Nor have thee slave for my sake.'

THE KENTUCKY WOMAN'S SONG OF THE SHIRT.

Air—' The Dumb Wife.'

We work for brave and true ;
'Tis but little we can do,
But with love our hearts are all rich, rich, rich.
We'll not let tired fingers rest
Until every captive guest
By our willing hands is drest—Quick ! Let us ' stitch,
stitch, stitch ! '

Ah ! we work with our might,
For we labor for the right,
And with love our hearts are all rich, rich, rich.
Then away despair, that gnaws
The heart of the good cause.
Captives, be of good cheer ; 'tis for you we stitch,
stitch, stitch.

We work for those who pine
For sweet freedom's seething wine,

And with love our hearts are all rich, rich, rich.
    They have done their best afield,
    Awhile proved themselves our shield;
Gratefully now for them we work—Quick! Let us
    stitch, stitch, stitch!

    Now, in the darkest hour
    May the captives never cower,
Know with love our hearts are all rich, rich, rich.
    They are honored here and blest,
    Counted as our brave and best;
We work for them as for our brothers—Quick! Let
    us stitch, stitch, stitch!

    And while our ' fingers fly '
    Earnest prayers are mounting high,
For with love our hearts are all rich, rich, rich.
    And faith says when weapons fail,
    Fervent prayer shall most avail.
Then for the captives let us pray while we stitch,
    stitch, stitch!

'SPARE US, GOOD LORD.'

Written while —— was playing 'Lurlei.'

By Thy sad Passion, hear us,
Send living hope to cheer us;
    Spare us, good Lord!

By Thy memory of scorn,
Help us who are so forlorn;
    Spare us, good Lord!

By remembrances of woe,
Lay our proud oppressors low;
    Spare us, good Lord!

Not that we deserve of Thee
Aught but death and misery ;
    Spare us, good Lord !

But our faith is very strong
That Thou wilt not favor wrong ;
    Spare us, good Lord !

Bad men think Thou wilt not mark
Those they threw in dungeons dark ;
    Spare us, good Lord !

Bring them to their homes once more,
Law and Liberty restore ;
    Spare us, good Lord !

'UNCLE SAM.'

Air—'Nelly Bly.'

Uncle Sam ! Uncle Sam ! De way you take is wrong ;
You'll nebber bring us back agin by cruel war and
    long.
Putting de women under lock, and knocking chil'ren
    down,
Case they hurrah for Jeff Davis, will 'kill' you, 'I
    be bound.'
Chorus.—Heigh, Uncle ! Ho, Uncle ! you jist bear
    Sambo ;
If it's money you want to make, you must to your
    home go.
Heigh, Uncle ! then Uncle ! We'll jist come to you,
And give you work, 'pay you twice' for all dat you
    can do.

Uncle Sam hab a voice like an old growling bar ;
It frightens women in de house and chil'ren ebry-
    whar.

But we, big men, nebber fear no sich voice as dat;
We tinks de men dat frighten gals will run like a
    wild cat.
Chorus.—Heigh, Uncle! Ho, Uncle! you jist hear
    Sambo, &c.

Uncle Sam, you's afeard ob pris'ner in de bed;
Won't let women go to him—fear'd dey'd put in his
    head
A way to get to Washington and put you in de jail
Den, Uncle Sam, I guess you'd like to get a long
    ' leg-bail.'
Chorus.—Heigh, Uncle! Ho, Uncle! you jist hear
    Sambo, &c.

Uncle Sam! Uncle Sam! now don't you look so
    glum,
We won't hang you; you's jist fit for Lunatics'
    Asylum.
De man who jistifies Butler ain't got no sense nor
    heart,
But in a war 'twixt heaven and hell he would take
    Satan's part.
Chorus.—Heigh, Uncle! Ho, Uncle! you jist hear
    Sambo, &c.

Uncle Sam! Uncle Sam! know down South we are
    men;
We will put you and Butler too in 'propriate pig-
    pen,
For we's de chivalry who fights for women and
    oppressed,
And you as their grim tyrant stand 'fore all de world
    confessed.
Chorus.—Heigh, Uncle! Ho, Uncle! you jist hear
    Sambo, &c.

'KENTUCKY TO THE RESCUE.'

Air—'I've something sweet to tell you.'

Kentucky to the rescue,
  For we are needed now;
I know our heart was always true,
  Though shrouded was our brow.
But Yankee hands a veil had flung
  Before our guileless trust,
And they have freedom's death-knell rung,
  So rule *them* now *we* must.

Our hands were folded in calm sleep,
  Induced by Northern drug;*
No more we sleep while brothers weep,
  And Yanks their shoulders shrug.
The giant has awakened now,
  Knows he has been aggrieved;
The Yankees must decamp, or bow
  To those they had deceived.

But all revenge we are above,
  That is too mean a game;
We'll conquer by both might and love—
  Unstained must be *our* fame!
Kentucky owns no coward son,
  Who shrinks from death in war;
But when the victory is won,
  The foes our brethren are.

Lincoln the False has 'had his day,'
  Because his faith is wrecked;
Davis the True we now obey—
  A man whom all respect.
And now, brave boys, fling up your hats,
  And rend with shouts the air;
Kentucky will give 'tits for tats;'
  Deceivers, now beware!

    * The 'neutrality' policy.

O gallant Morgan, 'tis to you
    Our hearts the soonest turn!
You laugh at the ' Red, White, and Blue '—
    Knock down the whole concern.
Hero true, women never fear,
    And gallant men admire;
But our invaders dread to hear
    Each night a sudden ' Fire!' *

Most of Kentucky's braves have gone
    To battle-fields afar;
But some remain who'll yet adorn
    The annals of the war.
Come back, lost brothers! you may earn
    Fame on Kentucky fields;
We'll join you, and all will learn
    Kentucky never yields.

June 7, 1862.

THE APPROACHING BATTLE NEAR RICHMOND, VIRGINIA.

Ah! hovers over them
    The gaunt war-demon fell;
Black cloud for diadem;
    Cannons' roar, as a bell
Calls many to their doom:
    Tolls for the parting souls,
The young, still fresh with bloom
    Of manly, fervid youth;

* A few days since there was a report that Morgan was coming to Bardstown; at night a guard was stationed at the door of every Southern sympathiser (nearly all of the respectable men, I understand), and ordered to shoot at the first head protruded from door or window. At Lexington and Frankfort, on hearing similar reports, all roads leading to them were guarded.

And for the good it tolls
   A requiem of peace:
Freedom is theirs in truth.
   In heaven invaders cease
To deluge homes with blood,
   And justify their crimes
By howls of loyalty.
   Heaven's ears are not so dulled
They cannot tell the chimes
   Which ring infernally
Of earth's cupidity.

O God! march with our men,
   Who fight for their birthright
Of blessed liberty!
   We are as one to ten;
But if Thy presence bright
   Will lead our armed hosts,
We'll march triumphantly
   To meet the vaunting foe.
We'll scorn their savage boasts
   To make us their dumb slaves;
Aye, we will all forego
   For liberty and right.
Better the freemen's graves
   Than heritage of slaves!
The North trusts in her might,
   Her resources of wealth;
But we trust in Thine arm,
   Thy hate of wrong and stealth.
Oh, shield him, Lord, from harm
   Who turned from council-board
To give himself to Thee;*
   His hand is now stretched toward
Thee, Guardian of the free.

June 1862.

* President Davis was lately confirmed.

GENERAL JACKSON IN THE VALLEY OF THE SHENANDOAH.

Air—'Dandy Jim.'

The clouds were heavy o'er our land,
And darkest o'er the brave, true band
That gathered Richmond to defend
From foreign armies, that intend
To spread their hated Stripes and Stars
Above our thirteen Stars and Bars.
And we were sad, for some must fall
Who were to many hearts their all.

But when the tempest darkest seemed,
Above our hosts a meteor gleamed:
Milroy and Schenck it glittered o'er,
And the invaders fled through gore.
The meteor then passed on to Banks,
And made the Yankees play fine pranks
At Front Royal and Winchester;
Goodie! But there was a great stir.

Fremont was 'big man' at Cross Keys,
But when the meteor comes he flees.
At Port Republic General Shields
Thought, 'I'll see how the meteor yields
To generalship of which I boast,
And then I'll be the Yankees' toast—
Whew! what a great man I shall be
If I can make this meteor fiee.'

No doubt each foreign general thought,
'Oh! I shall play a famous part
In conquering these free-born men.
The Southerners I'll beat. What then?
Then in the North I'll rule the roast.'
Jackson was quiet, did not boast
That the invasion could be balked;
Perhaps he prayed while others talked.

Milroy and Schenck, Fremont and Shields,
Were to pass from victorious fields
Over our bodies to Blue Ridge.
Thought Jackson, 'Their trip I'll abridge;
They cannot go to Richmond yet,
For first a whipping they must get,
And then we'll see if they will run
Towards us, or back to Washington.'

M'Clellan is afraid to strike;
What if the meteor should like
To flash awhile athwart his hosts?
He promised Richmond soon to take,
Knew not of Jackson in his wake.
Jackson, be still, you're not polite,
To put your guests in such a fright.

THE FAITH OF THE SOUTH.

God is the weak man's arm
    We cannot feel despair;
But check our vain alarm
With this ennerving thought,
    That God is surely where
He's trusted to the most.
Not of our power we boast,
But hope, O God! Thou art
The leader of our host.

A THANKSGIVING FOR VICTORY.

Air—'The Watcher.'

Let the church-bells anthems peal,
    Glad but low;
God hath seen our warriors kneel,
    Known their woe.

He hath heard each broken groan,
 Felt their trust ;
Doomed our foes from His high throne—
 They are dust.

When with fast, in faith we prayed,
 They'd deride ;
Boasted God would never aid
 Slavery's side.

Puritans ! They little thought
 God could see
They had set their haughty heart
 Slaves to free,

Only that they might enslave
 Millions more ;
Bury in fair freedom's grave,
 Steeped in gore,

Brotherhood and truth and right,
 Wealth to gain.
When the rich men die in flight,
 They'll retain

Orphan's portion, widow's dower—
 How they raved !
God hath spoken and they cower.
 We are saved.

Let the church-bells anthems peal,
 Glad but low !
For the Christian heart must feel
 For the foe.

Right hath triumphed ; we rejoice ;
 Give God thanks !
But the publican's low voice
 Thrills our ranks.

Naught but grief and misery
Were our due ;
Mercy pleaded ! we are free.
God is true.*

THE HERO'S DREAM.

Brig.-Gen. J. H. Morgan was so lionised in Kentucky that he often suffered for his fame. The incident recorded here took place at Lamenesburg. When he awoke and the tavern-keeper told him, he said, 'I dreamed of angels' visits.' It was this answer I intended to rhyme, but my muse willed otherwise.

Weary from his long toil
To free his native land,
And sick of the turmoil,
E'en of his gallant band,
He turned aside and begged that he might sleep,
If he but for awhile could quiet keep.

Ah ! what could satisfy
The longing of his heart
For one glance of the eye
That once with love was fraught,
But now slept cold and dead beneath the sod ? †
What is earth's fame to one beneath God's rod ?

He smiled benignantly
On those who pressed around,
But man's eye cannot see
Fires hidden 'neath the ground ;
Such burn the sufferer's life away e'en while
He seems contented and on all doth smile.

* To His promise to answer prayer.
† Gen. Morgan was always a lover-husband. One of his most intimate friends told me, that when alone with Mr. and Mrs. Morgan, she had often seen him make his wife drink from the glass he would use, and put his lips just where hers had been. It is said that since the war he has often visited her grave.

He slept and dreamed—oh, bliss !
   He pressed a well-known head
Close to his breast to kiss
   Lips that had long been dead.
And he was happy, for he sat beside
One who had been for many years his pride.

What now was it to him
   That his voice could command,
E'en for his slightest whim,
   Lives of the bravest band,
That fight our second war for liberty ?
She was by him; no glory could he see.

But even while he slept,
   On noiseless tiptoe came
Women who long had kept
   Within their hearts his name,
To keep alive their flickering, pale hope
That the harsh yoke of despots might be broke.

But one look did they take,
   Then made a whispered prayer
That, for their freedom's sake,
   Morgan might be God's care :
Comfort they gathered gazing on his face,
It was so full of love's unselfish grace.

He'll not forget his State,
   Beguiled by far-off fame ;
He'll save her from the fate
   He shudders but to name.
While she lies bleeding, bound to tyrants' car,
Her piteous cry will all his glory mar.

In his most blissful sleep,
   His country's woe forgot—
Her shadows could not creep
   Over the husband's lot.
The vision passed away, and he awoke,
And started up to feel Kentucky's yoke.

THE SOUTHERN WAGON IN KENTUCKY.

Air—'Wait for the wagon.'

Some Southern wit, deriding, said they must take
    up behind
The old Corncracker State, because at first she was
    too blind
To jump in wagon that Jeff drove and soak her land
    in gore.
Ah! she tried Yankees to beguile and was deceived
    much more.

Then told Kentuck that Davis said that she was surely
    right
To send provisions to the South and arms and men
    to fight;
But that they had more land than they could at that
    time defend,
And that the best thing she could do was South her
    men to send.

But all the while Kentucky sent her arms and
    warriors out
The Yankees theirs were bringing in; and, as with-
    out a doubt,
The canting Northmen always beat when craft is in
    the game,
For every man that we sent South a dozen Irish
    came.

Kentucky nothing had to gain by jumping in this
    war,
But she would ne'er consent to fight with men who
    brethren are.
So she will be the Cocles of this war of liberty,
And will destroy the bridge behind retreating enemy.

Kentucky gave the greatest gift the South has ever
    had,
For she gave it a President to make its great heart
    glad.
Johnston and Buckner, Breckinridge, the Johnsons,
    Hood, are ours ;
When her best fighting men are South is't strange the
    old State cowers ?

Oh ! send her back her valiant sons and all the arms
    she's given,
And then you'll see the foreigners will very soon be
    driven
Over the border, and then we can true elections hold,
For our elections are controlled by guns and not by
    gold.

But, oh ! if you have hearts of men, do not insult the
    State
Who's folded in a tyrant's arms she loathes with
    deadly hate ;
But bayonets are at her heart, and gags within her
    mouth,
And her best warriors and arms she has sent farther
    South.

Chorus.
Drive up the wagon,
The Secession Wagon !
We'll sit by Davis' side,
We're longing for a ride.

CAVALIER AND ROUNDHEAD.

Will he never come again,
    Come into my waiting arms ?
I am tired of common men,
    Feasting fancy on the charms

Of our Southern chivalry.
  Ah! how stale seem chatterings
Of the beaux I have to see!
  Solitude oftenest brings
Pictures that I love to paint
  Of my faithful cavalier.
Good as Louis, surnamed Saint,
  Fearful of a woman's tear,
Scornful of an armed host,
  Pitiful to suffering;
Never stooping to a boast
  Of the fame his brave acts bring;
Proud of only others' deed,
  Eloquent in others' praise,
Scarcely conscious of his meed,
  Saying that he but obeys.

Cavaliers are living yet—
  Calm not boastful, meek not vain,
Fighting not that they may get
  Wealth, or power, or other gain;
But to liberate oppressed,
  To maintain their country's laws,
Stand before the world confessed
  Champions of a righteous cause.
Dragon they have got to fight,
  Which was born in Yankee land;
In fanatic's armor dight,
  Guide of Puritanic band,
It has no sins to reckon,
  'Twill wash Southern conscience clean;
Valiant when it does not run,
  Brave enough ere foes appear,
But forgets the sufferings
  And the needs of those at home;
It some patent 'cure-all' brings,
  Made by Puritanic tome;

Says it, 'Swallow all, I say.
   In Don Quixote you believe;
Only pray for what I pray;
   Laugh with me, grieve when I grieve.
My foes I throw in prison,
   Nor give them a thought again;
Where I go there goes the sun—
   I'm the greatest of all men.

GRANT'S LITANY CHANGED TO SUIT MY FEELINGS.

Air—'Spanish Hymn.'

Savior, when in dust to Thee
Low we bow adoring knee,
When repentant to the skies
Scarce we lift our streaming eyes,
Oh, by all Thy pains and woe,
Suffered once for man below,
Jesus, look with pitying eye.
Victory! or we must die.

By Thy birth and early years,
By Thy human griefs and fears,
Feel the quiverings of our heart,
Whisper that our shield Thou art.
By Thy victory in the hour
Of Thy subtle foe's fierce power,
Jesus, to our woe draw nigh;
Cheer us with, 'Peace! I am by!'

By Thine hour of dark despair,
Nerve our souls Thy rod to bear;
By Thine agony of prayer,
Let us feel that Thou wilt care

O

For the friends for whom we pray,
Driven from their homes away.
Jesus, look with pitying eye ;
To our army, Lord, be nigh !

By Thy purple robe of scorn,
Succor us who are forlorn ;
By Thy wounds, Thy crown of thorn,
Let Thy pity in help dawn.
Let Thy Cross, and pangs, and cries,
For our nation's sins suffice.
Come, O Savior, at our cry !
At Thy feet a people lie.

By Thy deep, expiring groan,
Pity those who die alone ;
By Thy sealed sepulchral stone,
In hot strife soothe dying moan.
By Thy triumph o'er the grave,
Hear us, Christ, and haste to save.
Bending from Thy throne on high,
In the battle-hour be nigh.

A SOUTHERN GIRL'S SONG.

Air—'Come away, love.'

Come away, love, from my foes, love ;
   Come and seek a nobler cause.
Where, if there's not much to be made,
   Patriots are above gewgaws.
Your buttons, made of apple wood,
   True, will want the Northern glitter ;
But they'll keep warm a heart, love,
   That for a man is fitter.

Come away, love, from the foe, love,
   Or your ring I cast afar ;
Can I wed my father's foe, love,
   An abettor of this war ?

Which, if it does much longer last,
    Us of our all, but love, will rob;
But that's only for the free, love,
    Who e'er check each selfish throb.

Come away, love, from my foes, love.
    My brothers fight for freedom;
Will you dare to ask their sister
    To their tyrants' home to come?
I should pine away quite soon, love,
    Breathing the oppressors' breath.
Better die from broken heart, love,
    Than to live a 'living death.'

MAJOR-GENERAL S. B. BUCKNER'S CHIVALRY.

AN IMAGINATION.

Air—'Allan Percy.'

A Southern woman bowed in weeping stood,
Amid a crowd, unfeeling, selfish, rude;
The crown of sacred womanhood was gone—
She had been ruined while she stood forlorn.
        Crushed is she! Sad to see!

By some alluring draught* first stupefied,
Alas! she'd been beguiled to despots' side.
Her bravest sons then went to other lands;
The true who stayed were put in felons' bands.
        Don't condemn! Rescue them!

Helpless, forsaken, in her grief she prays,
'Sisters, help me win back my virgin days.
For sake of children banished from my side,
For sake of those who for their country died.
        Honor me! Set me free.

* The neutrality policy.
o 2

For sake of those who're left behind to pine,
Ye Southern sisters, send me some sweet sign
That I am not deserted in my pains,
For 'twas unconsciously I grasped my chains.
    On foes rushed ! Me they crushed !'

Some heard and scoffed; some coward hearts decried
The lonely woman in her sunken pride.
Then up rose one of noble form and mien,
A braver champion is seldom seen—
    How true ! Hearts he drew !

He bears sure marks of noble gentleness,
A man the mourner looks on, but to bless.
For small-souled men full is he of disdain,
E'en as of pity for hearts bowed in pain.
    Courage wins ! Hope begins !

With a wave of his hand he hushed the scorn
That cowards dared to point at one forlorn ;
So loving was his smile, so brave his eye,
There was not one who would his word defy.
    He is strong ! Woe to wrong !

' Buckner !' was whispered by the silenced crowd,
And many learned their petty scorn to shroud
Before his truth !* With thrilling voice he cried—
' This woman is my mother ! I'm her pride !
    For I'm true ! What are you ?

' It is no fault of hers that Yankee lied,
Beguiled the guileless to his heartless side ;

---

* Had our great men, Breckinridge, Buckner, Preston, Marshall, Simrall, and others, stayed in Kentucky and aroused the people by speeches, &c., we would be free, I think; but our land would be a howling wilderness, for we have not the natural protection dear, noble Virginia has. As it is, Kentucky has done *far* FAR more for the South than it ever did for her. How many thousand prisoners have we saved from perishing ?

Incapable of acting a deceit,
'Twas her misfortune that the Yankee beat.
    Her you blame ! His the shame !

' Now, when she sees that she has been deceived,
She's stupefied—of half her power bereaved ;
And calls upon her children for their aid—
He is unworthy son who'll now upbraid.
    His fame's dim ! Blame's for him !

' I am no coward son to hide my eyes ;
He is a bastard who can't sympathise
With grief of one whose borne him in her arms !
Who mocks a mother all her children scorns.
    She is mine ! She doth pine !

' He is a fool who scouts his mother's name,
Aiming to raise his on the roll of fame.
A parent's anguish fills the air we breathe—
Alas ! that we should let our mother grieve !
    To her haste ! No time waste !

' Scorn for the wretch who lets a mother weep !
Her voice fills the night air, I cannot sleep.
Arise ! and come with me, ye who are men !
We'll gather round our mother's knee again.
    She is ours ! and she cowers !

' If she's betrayed we are not without blame.*
Who was there to protect her sacred name
When we, her bravest sons, whose arms were strong,
Left her in all her helplessness to wrong—
    What to gain ?—South's disdain.'

' That is unjust,' was spoken in the crowd;
We did not leave her till she had avowed,
That on the Union she would not make war,
And us from further struggle would debar.
    Avenged we ! Her chains see ! '

  * Not as Confederate soldiers, but as Kentuckians.

Said noble Buckner—he appeared grand then—
' At that time she believed the words of men,
Who guaranteed she should a neutral be.
She was deceived—not hers the infamy :
    Guilt is theirs which she bears!

' But when the despot saw her sons divide,
He took away her weapons ; then she cried,
" That is not fair."   He riveted her chain ;
And now she half-stunned lies, quite dumb with pain,
    For us prays ! No delays !

' Who is a man, arise and follow me !
Who hates his mother, let the bastard flee !
The man who his own State can thus betray
To any other may the traitor play.
    I am true ! What are you ? '

WHERE MY HEART IS.

Air—' My heart's in the Highlands.'

My heart's with our brave men, my heart is not here,
For wherever I look, there Dutch soldiers appear ;
And they prowl round our homes, insult us, and scorn
The weak whose protections to battle have gone.
How long must we wait ere our brave men will come,
March home to the sound of the fife and the drum ?
Ah ! no lover's sweet tones were ever so dear
As music would be which would tell us they're near.

It seems that e'en now there is borne on the breeze
The war-note which tells us our enemy flees ;
But no time has he now to insult and to fright—
Our protectors so near, our joy's at its height.
We've wept through long nights, thinking we were
   forgot,
Left lonely and helpless to vassals' hard lot.
Forgive us, O God ! for Thou art ever near,
And Thy presence links us to those who are dear.

'NOW'S THE DAY AND NOW'S THE HOUR.'

Inscribed to Lieut.-Col. J. W. Bowles, 2nd Regiment Kentucky
Cavalry, by request of a friend of his boyhood.

Air— ' Bruce's Address to his Army ; ' some lines of it retained.

Old Kentuck, whose sons have bled
Where the bravest men have led,
Never known what 'twas to fear
    Foemen's threat or gun ;
Rally now at Morgan's call ;
Nobly live, or if we fall,
Consecrated are we all,
    Heroes every one !
        Chorus.
Now's the day, and now's the hour !
See the cloud of battle lower ;
See approach false Lincoln's power.
    Death, or slavery !

Who will be a traitor, knave ?
Who will fill a coward's grave ?
Who so base as be a slave ?
    Let him turn and flee !
Who for his own rights and law
Freedom's sword will bravely draw,
Let his body be the bar
    To the enemy !
    Chorus.—Now's the day, &c.

By oppression's woes and pains,
By our friends in cruel chains,
We will gladly drain our veins;
    But they shall be free !
Bow no longer to the foe ;
Base submission brings but woe.
    Make the despots flee !
    Chorus.—Now's the day, &c.

Gallant Morgan comes to free
Those who'll strike for liberty.
We are tired of slavery ;
  Let us share his fame !
At the head of bravest band,
He has come to free his land
From the foreigners who brand
   Her proud cheek with shame.
    Chorus.—Now's the day, &c.

Hear the noble Morgan cry,
'Armed are we to fight or die;
Let true patriots reply
  Soon to our appeal ! '
For the love of our dear State,
Rally, men, ere it's too late ;
No more can Kentucky wait—
  Let her tyrants feel !
    Chorus.—Now's the day, &c.

'WHAT TIME IS THIS FOR DREAMING?'

What time is this for dreaming,
 When hearts are breaking round ?
Me, I'd not have love's gleaming
 Within my spirit found.
Deep in Time's snowy bosom,
 Grasped stedfastly by fate,
Rest thee, love, and be thou dumb !
 War is my spirit's mate.

TO MR. VALLANDIGHAM.

O Chatham* of our day, to thee I turn,
While my sick heart with freshened strength doth
 burn,

* Since writing the above I have seen Mr. V. compared to
Lord Chatham.

To think that in a land where all seems base,
There is one to redeem the Northern race.
I honored you when you stood by the side
Of Breckinridge, Kentucky's hope and pride!
I honored more when his grand mind was gone.
Still one in Congress would I could not scorn.
Vallandigham, I know thy pulses thrill
As his of old who fought a monarch's will;
But harder task was thine than Chatham knew:
What was King George* to Lincoln and his crew?
Dost thou remember how, in boyhood's days,
Thy heart would bound to utter Chatham's praise?
Ah! so in days to come will Southern youth
Honor Vallandigham, the man of truth.
One Northern name in my betrayed State
Is ne'er received with sneers of scorn and hate.
Our servants† have betrayed us, have bound on
Shackles that we have borne with sullen scorn,
Hoping the time might come when such as thou
Would crush them to the earth.   Oh, giant, bow
Thyself in anger now! the Union shake;
O'erwhelm the traitors in a grand outbreak
Of righteous zeal!   Be Chatham to the end;
And the betrayed will claim thee as a friend.
No higher praise can I find in my heart.
I, Southron, bow to thee; worthy thou art
To be enshrined where only Chatham dwells;
Thou art a foe who a foe's hatred quells.

---

* But King George was devoted to Chatham.
† Congressmen and State legislators.   This was written before
Messrs. Pinell and Wickliffe had taken their present bold stand.
I believe George Pinell is our only Congressman who has never,
by any vote, betrayed the pledge given or implied at his election.

A TRUTH SPOKEN IN JEST.

Inscribed to Private ——, 2nd Kentucky Cavalry, who was
wounded in a fight at Paris, Kentucky.

Air—'Old Rosin the bow.'

The time was, I said 'I won't marry,'
    But oh! how could I then have e'er thought
That heroes of old whom I longed for
    Again in this life would take part?

I've 'cried my eyes out,' over novels;
    So I could not see every-day men,
But on moonlight nights oft desired
    That chivalry might live again.

And then I said 'Oh! but I'd marry
    A mild hero, distinguished in fight,
Who for some true, chivalrous action
    On fierce battle-field was made knight.

' I'd be proud to lean on a hero
    Who was knighted by tap of a sword,
To free oppressed, succor the weak,
    And love to one damsel afford.'

Ah! little I thought then that Morgan
    Would old chivalry soon bring to life,
And that I ere long would be wishing
    A 'horse thief'* ask me for wife.

I know not where else I can find one
    Who's so gentle in word, brave in deeds,
Who so scorns the forlorn to affright,
    As one who goes where Morgan leads.

* So Yankees who impress horses call Morgan's cavalry.

Here the blue coats are fright'ning us girls,
    And consider they're valiant heroes
When they put a woman in prison,
    And treat peaceful men as armed foes.

O Morgan! you've promised to succor
    All poor maidens alone, in distress;
I have no protector; oh, send me
    A cavalier my life to bless!

The one whom I ask for was knighted
    On battle-field of old Kentuck,
As he strove to rescue from thraldom
    Our birthplace by showing his pluck.

I hear that his badge is a scar—
    Yankees say he's disfigured for life;
But Southron girls think he's so handsome,
    He can very soon get a wife.

July 31.

VANGUARD OF OUR LIBERTY.

Air—'Boy's wife.'

The Yanks were sure that we were theirs,
Submissive prey of the Northern bears,
So by their hug they'd strangle us,
And thus put an end to freemen's fuss.

Chorus.

    Vanguard of our liberty
    Is brave Morgan's cavalry;
    They're the men the Yankees fear,*
    The champions brave Kentucky holds dear.

---

* Morgan's men ought to be honored, if they are not the vainest of men. Less than a thousand will start on what the Yankees call a raid; and all Kentucky Yankees, Indianians,

Oh ! ev'rything they'd ' nicely ' planned ;
Ev'ry brave freeman they had banned
By tyrants' ' look,' fanatics' ' hell,'
To lie and rot in a loathsome cell.
  Chorus.—Vanguard of our liberty, &c.

But our brave Morgan came along,
And the Yankees sang another song,
' Irish in front, we in the rear,
Much to be pitied, dying with fear.'
  Chorus.—Vanguard of our liberty, &c.

They sent a man with a rare name,*
To let our rescuers know they claim
The power to do just as they please
With freemen who scorn their high decrees.
  Chorus.—Vanguard of our liberty, &c.

Their General was afraid to fight
Morgan's main force, and so they were right
To turn aside after a few
Of our brave defenders' daring crew.
  Chorus.—Vanguard of our liberty, &c.

Their thousands our hundreds might attack,
Without a fear that they'd have to back ;
So valiantly they rushed down on
The little band that smiled in scorn.
  Chorus.—Vanguard of our liberty, &c.

and Illinoisians, are straightway frightened out of their wits.
A United States officer in Louisville said he believed he was
the only Union man in that city who slept the Sunday night
after the fight at Lebanon.

 * Brig.-Gen. A. C. Smith had command of the United States'
forces. There were three Colonels with their regiments, Capt.
Glass of Cincinnatti with his men, home guards, and everybody
they could get to follow, went in pursuit of Gen. Morgan.
Smith took good care not to let his ' horse thieves' get too close
to Gen. M.'s, but turned aside after two or three hundred men
under Capt. Bowles, who was surprised at Cynthiana, but not-
withstanding the great odds escaped with eight wounded and
fewer killed.

Yanks killed a few and wounded more,
But our men got off, and then Yanks swore,
To think they'd come so far for naught;
Their thousands our hundreds had not caught.
        Chorus.—Vanguard of our liberty, &c.

The lesson by this they should have learned
Was our brave chivalry well had earned
The right to old Kentucky's fame—
That when once aroused she is always ' game.'
        Chorus.—Vanguard of our liberty, &c.

A SOUTHERN MOTHER'S LAMENT.

The head that lay upon my breast—
O God! elsewhere it findeth rest.
The little child I lulled to sleep
Sleeps without me, the while I weep.
The warm hands that used mine to clasp
My restless ones no more will grasp.

The little feet that used to run
Beside me all day in the sun,
Left me to fight for liberty.
O God, now he'll be brought to me!
His comrades hailed him to the field;
Freedom called him to be her shield.

Willing was he for her to fall—
O God! his God! Thou knowest all!
I, restless, toss the feverish night
Away, and dread more coming light;
And sleepeth he so quietly,
He will not turn from enemy.

O God! is my heart cold and dead
That I can lie upon this bed
While he is with the enemy?
Thank God, when he died he was free!
I know he ne'er will suffer more
For the great cause. My heart is sore;
Oh, yes! my heart is crushed and worn,
His breast by Yankee bullets torn.

O God! great God! he was my pride,
And there is none on earth beside
So precious to my widowed heart.
My child! my darling! can we part?
It seems thou must come back to me,
Or else I must go after thee.

On yesterday I felt thee near;
Thou could'st not see me shed a tear.
I thought thou had'st come back to soothe
The pangs that e'en thou can'st not move.
O God! he was my child and pride.
I live, and he for freedom died!

He loved me, but his country more.
I never thought he'd go before
Me to the dark and silent land.
Not so! he lives with hero-band.
He'll never die: my darling lives,
Where God both peace and freedom gives.

On earth he could have only one,
And of the South he was brave son.
O God! if I had been a man,
His life had ended as began,
By my heart! Then death could not part—
Oh, sex, how merciless thou art.

'IT MATTERS LITTLE WHETHER GRIEF OR GLEE.'

It matters little whether grief or glee
Is life's short portion set apart for me;
But God bless those who are to me most dear,
And put aside awhile this heavy fear
That in grim tyrants' blood-dyed hands may fall
My brothers brave, whom hopes of freedom call
To give up all their earthly ease and wealth.
To think they had to go away by stealth*
From their own home to fight for liberty!
My Father, let them come again to me,
Shouting aloud, 'Oh, sister, we are free!'
And then how soon my woes will be forgot—
The patriot will not feel the woman's lot.

A YOUNG GIRL'S FOREBODING.

Ah! it is very hard
    To think my home may go
To satisfy rapacity
    Of a barbarian foe.

'Trembling in the balance'
    Are all my pretty things,
To which too tenderly
    My woman's spirit clings.

Treasures my hands have handled
    Till they seem human, too,
May desecrated be
    'Neath the Red, White, and Blue.

* Until the last day it will never be known how many
Kentuckians have lost their lives in attempting to reach the
Confederate lines. One young man said, 'I would start to the
army if I believed I should not be hung or shot before I got
there.'

The rooms in which I sit
  And work, or talk or pray,
May echo to the tramp
  Of men who fight for pay.

The pure white drapery
  Of windows and of bed
May fall about the forms
  Of monsters whom I dread.

And I may have to flee,
  Sick, desolate, and poor,
And brooding o'er the thought,
  I ne'er knew want before.

O God! I thank Thee now
  That I was never vain
Of wealth Thou gavest me;
  My pride could no one pain.

But oh! I have enjoyed
  Wealth's privileges great;
Remembrance of its joys
  No time can e'er abate.

My Father, grant that I
  To Thy will may resign,
Calmly and cheerfully,
  All I had thought was mine.

O God! preserve from taint
  My heart's most holy place,
For it is sanctified
  By love's peculiar grace.

August 2, 1862.

WORTHIER.

—— was shot in trying to escape from Rock Island.

My best friend dead ! yes ; shot that he did try
From prison to escape.   Ah ! he did die
Fearlessly as he lived, striving to flee
From bonds, that he might fight for liberty.
I wear them yet.   Worthier he than I.
Hunger and cold, danger made him defy.
'Twas manlier; he felt that death was by.
Better to risk life, than by inches die.
My hero-martyr, who died'st to be free,
Would that my heart was worthier of thee !
I've felt the spirit which would thraldom flee ;
But now I can feel only loss of thee.

'CHARMED LIFE.'

2 Kings vi. 16.

' Ah ! ours is such a little, half-armed band
Compared to those who fight to win our land !
How can we ever conquer in this war,
Our men so few ? '
                        ' Invisible some are.
Who knows but spirits of our Washington,
And those who fought with him, and freedom won,
Hover o'er us in the thick battle-smoke,
And lend the aid that we from Christ invoke—
Angelic ministry in the hot strife
Where patriots are said to have " charmed life." '

TO THE CONFEDERATE FLAG OVER OUR STATE HOUSE.

Air—' Oh, saw ye the lass?'

Float proudly o'er Frankfort, thou flag of my heart !
The dread of oppressors and hirelings thou art ;
Our eyes have grown weary of waiting for thee.
Too long have we waited, O Flag of the Free !
The men* who were pledged not to make war on thee
Betrayed us, and laughed that we'd thought ourselves
    free.
They bound us with shackles, and ere we could rise,
The gleaming of bayonets answered our cries.

Lives only our own we could lay down in scorn,
But we could not, we dared not, leave women forlorn ;
And so we have waited, have watched, and have
    prayed,
For sight of the Cross † that so long was delayed.
But now we will rise up like new men and strong,
And praise of brave SMITH be the theme of our song.
He has come ! he has come ! with Flag of the Free ;
No more shall our State Yankees' head-quarters be.

When freed from our tyrants, our children we'll teach
To lisp Kirby Smith in first essays of speech.
The flag he has planted on our State House dome
Gives him in the heart of Kentucky a home.

   September 6, 1862.

   * The legislators of Kentucky.
   † The Blue Cross battle-flag of the Confederacy.

BILL HOOSIER'S ADVICE TO THE HOOSIERS IN LOUISVILLE,

Three days after the battle of Richmond, Kentucky.

Air—'Sing, sing, darkies, sing.'

Why should Hoosiers spill their blood
To enrich Kentucky mud?
Corncracks will have their own land.
What's the use to make a stand?
> *Chorus.*
> Run, run, Hoosiers run!
> Don't wait till they fire a gun;
> Haste, haste, Southrons, run,
> If you want to see the fun!

We have beat great Kirby Smith;
Where we are's to him a myth.
He thought that he'd whip us out;
Wanted battle, found a rout.
> *Chorus.*—Run, run, Hoosiers run, &c.

He must think we've got no sense,
To defend at life's expense
Those who won't themselves defend,
Call our conqueror their friend!
> *Chorus.*—Run, run, Hoosiers run, &c.

What if we've a bounty got?
We have earned it in such hot,
Dusty days to flee so fast
As we have for three days past.
> *Chorus.*—Run, run, Hoosiers run, &c.

September 2, 1862.

'JOY, MY KENTUCKY!'

Joy, my Kentucky! thy night turns to morning,
Eager thou risest at Liberty's dawning; *
Clouds of the dark past are now fading in mist;
Their lives for our freedom Smith's brave men have
    risked.
With Buckner, chivalric, true-hearted, and brave,
Hope of the oppressed, Forrest hastened to save.
The women would crown Scott with flowers of the
    heart,
And with dear John C.'s † name each child's voice is
    fraught.

We thought that the South had deserted our State,
So callous she seemed to our desolate fate;
But since she has sent us such heroes as these,
To give her free flag to Kentucky's fond breeze,
Those banished by tyrants no longer need roam,
The Flag of the South is on our State House dome.
Joy, my Kentucky! we are not forgotten,
For Corn is the wife and queen of 'King Cotton.'

Joy, my Kentucky! thy shackles are riven;
Those who had bound thee, by thy sons are driven
Afar, though they thought we only would war
For States wherein none of our interests are.

---

* No one who was in Kentucky from July to September 1862
can fail to remember how the whole State thrilled at the prospect
of freedom; and we who were 'behind the scenes' knew that
want of confidence in the commanding General, and *his* ability
to hold the State, was the only thing that retarded volunteering.
An old gentleman, an oracle among his acquaintances, said,
'This campaign will be decided in favor of whoever reaches
Louisville first.' All prudent men shook their heads after
General Buell reached here, while General Bragg did nothing.

† A common way of speaking of the two celebrated Breckin-
ridges is 'our John C.'

Joy, my Kentucky! for thy Buckner is free;
Preston and Breckinridge hasten to thee.
Thy unselfish heart is rewarded at length—
Joy, my Kentucky! for great is thy strength.

A TWILIGHT PRAYER.

Written in the dark, Whit-Sunday morning.

God of battles, hear and save us
From the foes who would enslave us!
Without a warrant, Lord, from Thee,
They would be masters of the free.

O Thou, who did'st our fathers save
From less rapacious foe, and gave
To them the strength for victory,
From brute force we appeal to Thee.

Oh, save us, Lord, from the fierce power
That in a dark and hellish hour
Decreed our women's purity*
The plaything of their tyranny!

God of the helpless, hear their prayer!
While we fight make our wives Thy care.
Yes; we can leave them, Christ, to Thee,
Thou Guardian strong of purity.

Save them from demons' tyranny—
Thine eye has marked their cruelty;
Nor is there any wrong or sin
Where Thou as witness hast not been.

The 'battle is not to the strong,'
Or ne'er would those who suffer wrong
With the oppressor dare to vie;
We fear not force when Thou art by.

* Written after 'Beast Butler's' infamously famous order had
been promulgated in New Orleans.

INSCRIBED TO THE MEMORY OF CAPT. COURTLAND PRENTICE.*

(Morgan's Cavalry.)

Written after reading Mr. G. D. Prentice's (his father's)
beautiful obituary memoir.

O noble spirit! not in vain
Thy long three hours of direst pain!
Thine arm, uplifted high in fight,
Had urged men to defend the right!
Braver and longer fought they when
They thought upon the dying men
Who lay around in speechless woe,
The victims of invading foe.
O noble spirit! not in vain
Thy long three hours of direst pain!
The chivalry, that made a part
Of thy whole life, had well inwrought
The element of sacrifice,
And thou could'st close thy hero-eyes
To palms that waved beyond thy grasp,
Content to hold in mental clasp
The beau-ideal of thy life—
Thy country freed from the fierce strife
In which thou wert one of her braves;
O'er thee her Blue Cross flag she waves,
And chants a tender air and wild
Above her youthful, much-mourned child.
Yes, soldier, rest in long-lost calm.
She, waiting, holds victorious palm,
Which soon she'll wave above the graves
Of all our noble martyred braves.
O noble spirit! not in vain,
Thy long three hours of direst pain!

* Capt. Prentice was killed at Augusta, Kentucky.

The Christ who taught self-sacrifice
N'er turned away from contrite cries
Of him who suffered, victim brave,
For land he gladly died to save.
Oh! in the hours when death-waves roll
Their miserere o'er the soul,
The great Life-Pilot never passed
The heart which seeks an anchor fast.
Brave soldier, those who mourn thy fate
Should think how much more desolate
The pleasant home thy true heart loathed.
Yes; it was hard to be well clothed
And pampered while thy comrades fought
For what lay deepest in thy heart.
Better the silence of the grave
Than taunt of ' coward' to the brave!
Thy peers had won fair fame in fight;
Thou sorely chafed'st at the sight
Of State thou loved'st bound in chains;
Could'st thou be heedless of her pains?
No; chevalier of tear-blest fame,
Kentucky soon will chant thy name
With others on her roll of fame.
Not one has lost his life in vain
Who died to loosen tyrants' chain.

September **27, 1862.**

AN APPEAL.

Haste, Kentuckians! wait no longer;
Rally, and you will be stronger
Than you ever would suppose
While submitting to your foes.

Freedom is better far than health,
A nobler heritage than wealth.
Let no love of ease detain you,
Or free hearts will soon disdain you.

One would save his estate.   Would he ?
Him will we spurn when we are free.
One would gain a fortune. - Let him.
Our scorn will all such splendor dim.

Another wife and child must guard :
A true wife would refuse such ward
As brought her husband slavery,
For love's a twin to bravery.

True, all men cannot go to war ;
But let our State be on a par
With noble sisters that have given
Husbands and sons—their chains are riven.

Ye tremble at the tyrants' beck ;
Be bolder, men, or ye will wreck
Honor that should your children's be.
Choose for them—fame or infamy !

'HA ! HA ! THE FIGHTING, HA !'

Sung after the battle of Richmond, Kentucky.

Air—' Ha, ha ! the wooing, ha !'

Kirby Smith came here to fight !
    Ha ! ha ! the fighting, ha !
We Yankees are by far too bright
    To waste our time in war.
It's well enough to eat and sleep,
    While lolling in the camps ;
Fine fun to make women weep
    By showing ourselves scamps.

We Yanks stole, and we Yanks talked ;
    Ha ! ha ! the fighting, ha !
Kirby Smith came and we were balked
    In apple-orchard war.

And then we ran—it was too hard
    Such glorious fruit to leave;
Ah! were I but a great bard,
    I'd make e'en Corncracks grieve.

We Yanks came down here to feast;
    Ha! ha! the fighting, ha!
Kirby Smith came like some great beast,
    Our splendid times to mar.
If Kentucks had Ohio crossed,
    Just to get enough to eat,
And had all their plunder lost,
    Would they like to be beat?

We Yanks now have gotten thin;
    Ha! ha! the fighting, ha!
Because since Kirby Smith came in
    We've had to run so far.
Our corpses would not fatten hawks
    Since we've grown so very thin,
We weren't used to such long walks
    Till Kirby Smith came in.

Kirby Smith came here to fight;
    Ha! ha! the fighting, ha!
Surely he can't be very bright—
    He thought that we meant war.
A bounty is a splendid chance
    A patriot's heart to sell;
But won't pay men to advance
    When Southrons come pell-mell.

Smith brought infantry to fight;
    Ha! ha! the fighting, ha!
But it can't catch a blather's kite
    When Yanks and Dutch make war.
Two bodies can't stay in one place,
    So since Kirby Smith is here,
We will not leave one scapegrace
    To spoil Corncrackers' cheer.

We were sent Kentuck to guard ;
    Ha! ha! the fighting, ha!
We guarded many a poultry-yard,
    And on the pigs made war.
Kentuck has fed us long enough,
    It's time for us to go ;
But we'll take along a little ' stuff,'
    And thus we'll beat the foe.

Does Smith think to fight for it ?
    Ha! ha! the fighting, ha!
We'll wager he'll ne'er get a bit
    Of trophies of our war.
He'll never get one back again !
    Even horses cannot run
As fleetly as we Yankees when
    We hear a Southern gun.

A BETRAYAL.

Dallying on as fair a landscape
As the skies in beauty drape,
There reposed a guileless maiden ;
With freedom her soul laden.
On his knee beside her sank there
One whose face was very fair ;
And passionate his words, to prove
Unselfishly her he'd soothe.
But the love he thus asserted
She heard with eyes averted,
Because they eagerly were turned
After one for whom she yearned.
But the proud one in the distance
Never gave beseeching glance ;
And the friend who knelt beside her
To her dictum did prefer
Every question that concerned him.

Ah ! the longed-for one not caring,
Her courage was fast despairing ;
And he who knelt beside her saw
How her pride and love made war.
No longer then he urged his suit,
But turned sadly to his lute,
Mourning, as only to himself,
How he would give all his wealth
If he could only gain her heart
From whom some could willing part.
So he but asked that she would be
Aye from vows of wedlock free :
This promised she with meaning smile,
Never fearing lure or guile.
Wearied, she sadly sank to sleep :
Waited he until the deep
Sleep of exhaustion o'er her fell ;
'Ha,' then cried he, 'this is well.'
Then gilded chains he o'er her threw ;
Tightly round her hands he drew
Shackles that bore a padlock-heart—
Triumph true of Yankee art.
He other chains bound round her feet,
Fastened them as it was meet
To a mock form of liberty*—
Gold, as such a queen should be.
Softly he whispered in the ear
Of the maiden, ' Do not fear ;
I swear that you shall not be hurt :
Deftly are your limbs now girt.'

* The figure of Liberty on the U. S. gold coin. It is needless
to say, that the maiden slighted by the South and wooed by the
North is Kentucky.

'PATIENCE, PATIENCE, O MY SPIRIT!'

Patience, patience, O my spirit!
Only patience doth inherit
The great meed of victory.
Patience! we will yet be free.

Though the hope that lured us onwards,
Backward falling, disregards
Mangled hearts it trampled down,
Yet, my spirit, press thou on.

If not in, thou may'st look upwards;
Though man fails,* the heavenly guards
Are around us; they are more
Than the enemy before.

Man may leave us, God will never;
If we're faithful He will sever
Chains which wear our free souls through,
And our vigor He'll renew.

Tyrants' hands so long have bound us,
Despots' tools so long have ground us
Underneath their blood-dyed feet,
That our numb hearts are not meet

Yet to taste a draught of freedom.
But patience, spirit! She will come
Yet, and lay her hand upon thee,
Telling thee thy State is free.

Baptism of true blood may yet be
Needful for my dear Kentucky,
But when purified she'll rise
To the sphere of sacrifice.

* 2 Kings vi. 16. Written when I was forced to believe that
the Confederates had deserted us.

Patience, patience, O my spirit!
For thou can'st bear if God permit:
'As thy day thy strength shall be.'
Live on faith till we are free.

October 20, 1862.

GOD BLESS OUR PRESIDENT.

God bless our President,
  The hope of the free !
For since great Washington,
  No rival has he.
Quite untainted by pride,
  Though of him we're proud,
He yet seems not to hear
  Our compliments loud ;
Nor yet seems he to fear
  The outcries of wrath ;
He asks God what is right,
  And follows that path.

If I wished a favor
  'Tis to him I would go,
As the noblest feel most
  For those who're in woe.
Ah ! there's but one favor
  That I would demand,
It would be to ask him
  To think of my land.
But then this is needless,
  For he'll not forget
The hearts that pray * for him ;
  He'll rescue us yet.

* Probably, at the great majority of family altars in Kentucky,
President Davis is daily prayed for; and whenever you open a
Prayer-book, the chance is that in the prayer for the President
'United' is marked over, and 'Confederate' written in the margin

TO KENTUCKY.

By an advocate of States' rights.

I lay my heart upon thy breast;
   They who strike thee must pierce me first.
Invaders' tramp has not distressed.—
   As children whom my mother nursed,
Who've turned their backs upon their State.
O God! forbid such I should hate!

He who scorns thee dishonors me;
   My mother's blood fills ev'ry vein.
Let men hate me if they'll love thee;
   Would my blood could wash out thy stain!
If in the battle-field I fall,
   Ye Southern sons of Liberty,*
Know that to me the bitterest gall
   Was blame of State dearest to me.

MORGAN'S CAVALRY AND THE GIRLS.

Air—'Coming through the rye.'

If brave Southron meet our Morgan,
   Coming through Kentuck,
He's pretty sure to go with him,
   E'en for love of pluck!

We Corncrackers love our freedom—
   We'll have it soon or late;
The North can't always keep us down,
   The prey of Yankee hate.

Not that we cannot pray for Mr. Lincoln, as well as St. Paul
did for Nero, the oppressor of his people, but that we regard
Mr. Davis as our true (if not real) president.
  * This was written before the days of 'The Sons of Liberty.'

And of all men
There's none I ken
   So worthy of our trust
As he who first
Our shackles burst,
   Made tyrants ' bite the dust.'

True girls have said they will not wed
  The men who can refuse
To go with Morgan's Cavalry,
  For fear they'll get a bruise.
     They say to all
     The men who call,
      ' What ! are you still at home ?
     My lover's gone
     To greet the dawn
      Of freedom soon to come.' *

The fellow who thinks that he'll woo
  Kentucky's fairest maid,
Must join Morgan's Cavalry,
  Or else she will upbraid :
     ' I cannot wed
     Such a blockhead,
      Who scorns sweet liberty ;
     When the war's done
     I'll marry one
      Of Morgan's Cavalry.'

THE RECRUITING SERGEANT.

I am a Southern Recruiting Sergeant, oho !
The way that the ranks can be filled up I know.
I wonder what maiden has got spunk enough
To show that her heart is of true Southern stuff.

* I have heard this said of the young ladies of Georgetown,
Kentucky.   Honor to them !   As for our other towns, ' a word
to the wise is sufficient.'

Ho, maidens! come hither and listen to me;
Who of you a recruiting sergeant will be?
    Who loves noble Jeff most?
    ·Who makes Dixie her toast?
      'I! I! I! I!'
    I hear girls cry.

A Recruiting Sergeant I am, as I said;
But I find that men by the women are led.
So, ladies, be spry! I've work for you to do;
You've a chance now to prove who to Dixie is true.
If you are, not another man you'll receive
Who has no good reason why he does not leave
    His dear, sweet rocking-chair,
    Where he plays with his hair.
      O! O! O! O!
    How the men go.

KENTUCKY'S MOTTO.

On her Seal.

' United we stand, divided we fall.'
Rally, Corncrackers! Kentucky doth call
    Her children to rally,
    And on the foe sally.
The Yanks long enough have been 'pricks in our
    side;'
And over our hearts like demons they ride.

They gulled us and galled us till, in our despair,
We thought that our fate was in silence to bear.
    Now Davis says 'Rally!'
    Let's not dilly-dally;
He will not forsake us, that much we may know;
He is ready to help us expel our fierce foe.

'United we stand;' we have but one voice,
And that one proclaims Jeff. Davis our choice.
                Since our Washington's days
                No man merits such praise
As he receives from the heart of Kentucky.
Davis is ours; O Corncracks, we're lucky.

'Divided we fall.' Oh, yes! that we know;
And so as one man to Dixie we go.
                Those who will not submit
                Now Kentucky must quit.
We can do very well without them, I trow.
O Yankees, skedaddle, or to Jeff. Davis bow!

THE NEW FASHION.

Air—' Rory O'More.'

Make way there! Look out! A hare-brained hero
     comes.
Your loudest bugles sound! and beat, oh, beat your
     drums!
Ye white maidens, flee, and fair children, away!
No more must child of the doomed white dare to play
Bring out the great black race, refined Yankees' gods!
The heroes of Northern speech-makers and bards!
Fair skins and Greek statues have now 'had their
     day;'
Oh, knock them all down that new bronze statues may
Be set up on high, as the Yankee prefers:
The blackies are 'lions' now, white men are curs.
On the Washington monument much do I fear
They may put up Sambo or Cameron next year.
Upon the grand altar where freedom will die
Will great Lincoln in fine ebon effigy lie.

Q

THE CHURCH OF THE NORTH.

Inscribed to Bishop Hopkins, of Vermont.

Written during General Convention, October 1862.

In the midst of raging billows
Zion's 'harps hung on the willows,'
And, my limp nerves unstrung, I lay
Silently dying 'mid decay.

Clouds were very thick above me;
But darker still the blood-red sea,
While corpses rotted on the strand—
Marked on some foreheads was Cain's brand.

Ah! tightly folded were my hands
O'er bursting heart, like iron bands.
For why should I let love appear
When only curses it would hear?

So, broken-hearted, tired of life,
Those dearest to me lost in strife,
Where could I turn my failing eye
Without more longing soon to die?

Worn out, I lay me down to sleep;
Better for my heart worms should creep
About it when it cannot feel,
Than writhe to hear strange cannons peal.

And as it is my wont to kneel
Before sleep's hands my eyelids seal,
Though Northern winds howled fearfully,
I sought belovèd Mother's knee.

But it was dark, I could not find
My Mother-church, who was so kind
When I had been a happy child:
Had Satan e'en her heart beguiled?

Hides she her face when most I need
Cool oil poured in the wounds which bleed—
Which by my brothers' hands were made?
Or is she of the world afraid? *

My Mother deaf to wounded child!
The Savior's Spouse by war defiled.
I fell upon the blood-stained shore,
Asked God to make me bear no eor.

' Poor child,' one answered, ' do
Be quiet, and thou soon wilt hear
A flute-like, luring lullaby
Come o'er the mountains strong and high.

' Over broad plains and rivers deep
Thy Mother hastes.   Lie down and sleep.'
I was so tired I lay down where
I once had fallen in despair.

As a child doth a pillow hold,
My weak faith did a stone enfold ;
I wound my heart-strings round that stone,
Nor felt so desolate and lone.

I slept and dreamed—oh, fairest sight !
My Mother-church, in robe of white,
Sat on the stone that I had grasped ;
She leaned against a cross I clasped.

The billows, like fierce beasts of prey,
Dashed towards the rock on which I lay.
She looked above.   ' Peace,' some one spoke ;
The bloody waves in stillness broke,

---

* It was while reading some articles in a Church newspaper
that a fear stole over me that the sons of the Puritans, converted
by the sons of the Cavaliers and the Knickerbockers, might
prove too strong for the genius of the Episcopal Church. Besides,
I well knew what outside means were taken to intimidate the
General Convention, and how politicians at Washington were
striving, through her, to influence the intellect of the North.

Swiftly receded from the land
On which the rock-held cross did stand.
I smiled, thanked God, and looked around ;
Many the waifs upon the ground—

Hands that in brothers' blood were dyed,
Tongues that our Father had denied,
Eyes which had seen no form but self,
Hearts which had beat for only pelf,

Were stranded at my Mother's feet.
She gathered all with greetings sweet,
And hung as trophies on the cross
All that the Unseen would endorse.

I asked why these belonged to her ;
She answered that she did prefer
To keep her robe out of the sand
Of politics' polluted strand.

And, therefore, those wrecked by the war
Hastened to her, for she could bar
Its discords out, and let them rest
In quiet on their Savior's breast.*

I was awakened by soft strain,
Which made sweet music in my brain,
While my heart-beats the time did keep.
Michigan's bishop† called Christ's sheep,

---

* Very many Episcopal churches (one in my neighbourhood)
have been built up by members of other churches seeking refuge
from political sermons and prayers. A friend, influenced by the
articles referred to in the note on the previous page, exclaimed,
'If I can't find peace with you, where can I find it?' She had
left the church of which she was a communicant because she
could not endure the prayers, that would have been more appro-
priately offered to Moloch than to our Father.

† Calhoun said, in Congress, that the Episcopal Church was
the only power that could save the Union.—See Benton's *Thirty
Years in the United States' Senate.* The pastoral letter of the
Southern bishops says, 'A Church with whose action, up to the
time of separation, we were abundantly satisfied.'

Bade them beware of treason high—
Who wounds the Church doth God defy.
Chambers, Seymour, Mahan, Hunt, Mead,
To his sweet voice gave blessed heed.*

The Southern heart forgot one pang
To hear the Christ-tuned strain which rang
Above the cannons' horrid din,
Above the politician's sin.

Ah ! if these had been heard before,
Our land would not be dyed in gore ;
The Union's lost, the Church is saved,
Though politicians o'er it waved

War's firebrand ; they cannot set
On fire the Church.   We'll not forget
That the South owes the North a debt
Of love that she will pay back yet.

Our great heart swells with love for those
We count as friends among our foes—
Not friends in council or on field,
And not in either will we yield.

But when peace brings its longed-for calm
O'er Blue Cross flag we'll wave the palm,
And lay it at our Mother's feet,
And in her house as children meet.

*   *   *   *   *   *

* Messrs. Horatio Seymour and Washington Hunt, and the
learned divine Dr. Mahan, of New York, Judge Chambers, of
Indiana, and Rev. Mr. Mead, of Pennsylvania, were not the only
ones, by very many, who made noble speeches in the Convention,
which I made a fierce 'fire-eater' read ; he had declared there
was no religion in the land. He confessed he must except the
Episcopal, and so he has ever since spared her in his denun-
ciations. He never enters a church, but there is one he don't
hate—like Jefferson.

This I had sung, and then lay down,
Thanking God for my Mother's crown,
Which she bore high above the waves
Of politics and war-made graves.

But there rang in my head so strange
A discord I could not arrange
What meant the names that pained me so—
The ' evangelical ' * Brunot,

Hoffman and Goodwin, Welsh and Thrall.†
In vain did I my Mother call;
I felt that she'd forsaken me,
Heark'ning to others' jealousy.

Two shepherds pained me above all—
No more can some sheep hear their call,
For if they will bemire their feet
In politics, their Christ they'll cheat.

O God! hast Thou forgot us quite,
That few fanatics thus can blight
The noble name our Mother bore—
The one unstained by brothers' gore ?

In agony I struck my hand
Upon the coarse, unfeeling sand,
And said we'd cast our Southern heart
On one which no warmth could impart.

---

* I write this word not with a sneer but with a sigh. More-
over, if a Churchman introduces politics in his church, he is
sure to be ' low church.'
† I wish the above-mentioned gentlemen could have seen the
exultation made by members of other communions over their
speeches. We are not allowed to forget them. No doubt the
same jealousy at our rapid increase, from political causes, &c.,
acted upon the minds of these gentlemen by the cunning of men
who argued for patriotism. Which *is* of greatest importance,
God or the Union ? Some answer one, some the other.

'Nay, child,' one said, 'thou do'st us wrong;
Thou can'st not know how our hearts long
To soothe away mistakes and pride,
And win ye back to brothers' side.

We feel that those who would break down
Intrenchments which the sects rush on,
Degrade our Mother e'en as they
Who for Christ's sake His children slay.

They've wounded thee?   Trust but one hour;
Thy Mother, by her Savior's power,
Will rally from the cruel stroke
Which *by surprise* her quiet broke.'

Such words were sweet: I raised my head;
The demon, War, had vanishèd:
In the far North I saw a form,
Which grandly towered above the storm—

Vermont's good shepherd, high above
All party-spite, and full of love
For all for whom his Savior died.
Church of the South, in such confide.

[Bishop Hopkins is now presiding Bishop of the Episcopal
Church.—Ed.]

'THE NEXT TIME THAT BRAGG COMES THIS WAY.'

The next time that Bragg comes this way
I hope that he will come to stay,
For I am just at my wits' end:
Whene'er I meet a Yankee friend.

I'm so afraid he'll call out 'Bragg,'
And if he does I'd like to gag
The man who works our army so—
I wept enough when it did go.

At first I thought 'twas strategy
When Bragg from Frankfort took line-bee;
I said M'Clellan's art he'd learned;
My lips curled then—soon my cheeks burned.

I said that Bragg would change his pace,
And then the enemy he'd face;
Who thought he'd treat Kentucky so—
Just come to barter, and then go?

The Yankees don't treat her this way;
But when they come they come to stay.
Ah! we know this, and so we suit
Ourselves to circumstance—are mute.

Some thought our time had come to brag,
And they hung out the hidden flag;
Now their mistake they expiate
In pig-pens*—prudence came too late.

I think this would be a good thing,
Bragg's army to M'Clellan's bring;
Then Bragg will get to Richmond first,
In Washington Mac will be erst.

Send Preston, Buckner, Breckinridge,
And Yankees' walks we will abridge;
And they won't come here just to eat,
And run to show they can't be beat.

As Morgan's men don't care to eat,
And never run when they can beat,
As sleep they count a useless thing,
And live, like birds, upon the wing,

I think they would do very well
To come into our State, and tell
Us that they had come here to stay,
And not to brag and run away.

November 27.

* I can't think of a better name for Yankee prisons.

'ONLY ONE FELL.'

'The enemy was repulsed and only one fell; —— of ——.'—
Southern Newspaper.

' Only one fell,' and his name was told.
' Only one fell,' but him death could not hold,
For pearl gates ope'd to let him in,
Just rescued from bloodshed, and groans, and sin.

' Only one,' was shouted in hell,
' Are we cheated of now ; but ere they'll quell
Our own war of rapine and greed,
Souls will fly to hell like the thistle seed.'

' Only one,' and a mother shrieked,
That God all His vengeance on her had wreaked ;
Her son the bravest, he the best,
And he sleeps alone on the earth's cold breast !

' Only one,' and a father groaned,
And said, ' For ambition he had atoned ;
His staff was gone ; he was too old
To have such another good son and bold.'

' Only one,' a fond mother sighed,
' But he was the one who grew by my side ;'
' Only one,' and a sister wept
That o'er her pride death's dank chill had crept.

' Only one,' read a maiden fair,
And pressed her cold hands in quiet despair :
' Only one ;—but I have no more.
Only one ;—but my love-life is all o'er.'

VICTORY.

Written on hearing of the victory of Gen. Morgan at Hartsville,
Tennessee.

Oh, how I thrill in ev'ry nerve !
I, who for tyrants never swerve
A hair's breadth from what I think right,
Tremble like child in victory's light.
My country's victories are mine,
And a triumphant day doth shine
On my numb heart like summer sun,
While wildly doth my glad blood run.

CHRISTMAS EVE.

Christmas is here—time to be glad !
Alas ! I seldom am so sad ;
And bitter tears have fallen on
The cedar cross which will adorn
The rooms that we'll try to make gay,
In honor of Christ's natal day.

Give me some cedar for the clock ;
It struck the hours when Ma did rock
Upon her breast my brothers dear.
Where are they now ? Alas ! I fear
If I could know, I'd be more sad,
And Christmas is time to be glad.
Give me some bright vines for these frames,
Whose inmates looked upon our games
When we were children, one in glee—
Now we are one for liberty.
My heart tells me this Christmas Eve
My brothers sigh their arms to leave,
And hasten home the feast to keep ;
But they must sigh and I must weep.

O'er this door hang an ivy wreath,
For ere Lent comes may pass beneath
My brothers, worthy to be crowned.
They come ! They come ! Oh, joyous sound !
This we believe.   Our tyrants try
To brag when Southerner is by,
But we can see they are in fear ;
Soon our deliverers will be here.
Ere they'll have much more time to goad
Our helplessness, avenging sword
May free us from their cruel power.
If Christmas could wait till that hour !
I look upon mahonia cross
And shudder : what if brothers' loss
Should be the cross appointed me ?
' By Thy tears,' Savior, pity me !
' By Thy birth and early years,'
Have pity on a sister's fears !

For shame, my heart, so sad to be !
Think what thy Father's done for thee ;
When balls have fallen thick as hail,
His arms were as a coat of mail
To those whom He had made His care,
Thus answering a sister's prayer.
So rouse thee, heart, and gladly keep
The festival.   Know thy God can
Feel all thy woes, for He was man.

HEARING CANNON.

I feel as though in my own coffin laid,
List'ning to the last office that is paid
To what was once a throbbing, loving heart.
These cannon-booms with some death-knell are
    fraught.
Has Vicksburg fallen 'neath Thy wrath, O God ?
Ah ! then Kentucky feels Thy grievous rod.

She joyed to think one city could be held—
More fortunate than hers, which are compelled
To hold their peace in presence of their doom.
But we will wait, in patient faith secure
That Thou'lt not help men whose aims are impure.
All nations sin—as such pay penalty :
When this we've done Thou'lt grant us liberty.
I hear the shrieks of many hundred ghosts,
Although the moon smiles placidly to-night
Upon a world of graves and broken hearts.
The child who last year chatted on the knee
Of tender father now asks pleadingly
To whisper in the ear that heard no voice
But that of fame till it was called to God.

Another weeps in holy orphanhood,
For one who died that his son might be free.
Oh, child of such a parent! know thou hast
The honors of nobility that time
Nor envy cannot rob thee of.   Child of
The free, rejoice !
                      Child of the despot, flee
From bloody heritage ! scorn the base gold
Coined out of wretched hearts and agonies
Of death.   Cast down the blood-bought gold
At Jesus' feet lest it should curse thy life.

We, whom the war has visited and left
Unscathed, know not how we can give God thanks
Enough : perhaps our gratitude we best
Can show by giving most God saved for us
To cheer the poor, and to proclaim His name.

THE THIRTY-SEVENTH CONGRESS.

Now, isn't this Congress of ours something rare ?
It wants to see how much we poor fools can bear ;
It 'takes the oath' one day that white is but white,
And we bow to its wisdom, confounded quite !
But the next day it tells us that white is black,
And we can't doubt that—there are armies to back
Whatever the monkey-show chooses to say.
What matter ? It's only our conscience we pay
To keep up exhibition noble and rare.
Why, to scale the heavens I think it would dare ;
For it has now decreed the Bible is wrong
To pass slavery by as 'twere an ' old song,'
And the Bible is wrong in another thing—
It says we shan't steal; but then how could we bring
The war to an end if we're only to fight ?
We battle with women and old men for spite ;
The husband and strong sons who meet us afield
Will humiliate us by making us yield,
So the great monkey-show, with its wondrous brain,
Has made Confiscation the queen of its reign,
And old Abraham holds his honor so cheap
That if we believed him he'd feel himself piqued.
Why, any poor numbskull could ' stick to his word ;'
The keeper of monkeys is not so absurd ;
He has some paladins as wondrous as he,
And their funniest notion they call liberty.

'AULD LANG SYNE.'

A supposed song of Morgan's Cavalry on entering a Kentucky
town.

' Shall auld acquaintance be forgot,
    And not now brought to mind ?
Shall auld acquaintance be forgot,
    And days o' lang syne ? '

Chorus.

'For auld lang syne, our friends,
　For auld lang syne,
Give us your hands in kindness yet,
　For days o' lang syne.'

We gathered laurels in the South,
　And got our meed of fame ;
But still our hearts were in Kentuck,
　Thrilled fondly at her name !
　　Chorus.—'For auld lang syne,' &c.

And so we have come back again,
　To free you from your chains ;
'Twas not enough that we were free ;
　Our hearts bled for your pains.
　　Chorus.—'For auld lang syne,' &c.

Surely, you'll never be afraid
　Of your own sons and friends ;
We ask from you the cheering smiles
　Which love to bravery sends.
　　Chorus.—'For auld lang syne,' &c.

We never shrink from Lincoln's guns ;
　We fight for those most dear,
But heavily our hearts will throb,
　If you your best friends fear.
　　Chorus.—'For auld lang syne,' &c.

The boys may cheer for whom they please ;
　With boys *we* do not fight.
Women may wear red, white, and blue ;
　The weak *we* scorn to fright.
　　Chorus.—'For auld lang syne,' &c.

We have not come to tyrannise
　O'er those who do not fight,
We have come liberty to bring ;
　Injustice can't make right.
　　Chorus.—'For auld lang syne,' &c.

But ye who have Kentucky hearts
    Don't shame us by your dread;
Our lives we'll lay down for your sakes—
    Cheer the red, white, and red.
        Chorus.—'For auld lang syne,' &c.

THE COLONEL GILBERT.

The petty Cromwell of our State oppressed
Is Buckeye Gilbert, as must be confessed;
Between the Cromwells, first and second, though
There's a slight difference, as Corncracks know.
The first let men commit themselves before
He punished them; the second closed the door
Before we had had time to 'say our say,'
So, though not 'loyal,' we will martyrs play.
We would like much to try our game again,
But we're afraid he'd not molest us then.
I'd give a 'heap' to be in Dixie when
Gilbert is hissed as smallest of small men.
His masters have proclaimed Kentucky theirs,
And he has proved her soil rank 'rebels'* bears.
We cannot even be allowed to speak
Before some foreigner begins to squeak.
Gilbert has proved that we to Jeff would go
If we had more than tongues to fight the foe.

---

* I use the word 'rebel' as being the title applied to us by
the Lincolnites; but as the South owes no allegiance to the
North she cannot be in rebellion against her. Gilbert, with a
regiment (?) of Buckeyes, went to the theatre in Frankfort,
where the Democrats, *alias* Southerners, were going to hold a
Convention, and stationed themselves on the stage. As the pro-
ceedings of the Convention began, the curtain was drawn, and
the assembly dispersed at the point of the bayonet. Some said
we were going to have another Mayfield Convention; why did
not they wait and see?

England to hate of Cromwell owes her queen,
Kentucky needs no Gilbert now to wean
Her heart from servitude; but she'll accept
His service, hoping soon to pay her debt.

CHARLESTONIANS AND YANKEES.

The Yankees.
Ho! heigho! for Charleston, ho!
Nine grand ships make wondrous show.
Root of all sedition, she
Smoking ruins soon shall be.
Ho! heigho! for Charleston, ho!
Even now she wails in woe.

The Charlestonians.
God of mercies, hear our prayer;
Spare the land Thou mad'st so fair.
Like sea-waves, on rush the foe,
Breathing hatred, death, and woe;
Say to them, 'No farther go,
Or Thou'lt lay their proud heads low.'

The Yankees.
Ho! heigho! for Charleston, ho!
Fame, begin your blast to blow,
Strong and jaunty ships are ours;
Even now old Charleston cowers
As she sees us steaming up—
Goodie! how the sharks will sup!

The Charlestonians.
God of pity, shield us now,
At Thy footstool low we bow.
. With our mouths laid in the dust,
Only in Thy strength we trust.
Let Thy pity now decree
No sin is it to be free.

The Yankees.
One of our fine ships is lost,
Others are most madly tossed
On the waves, the sport of fate;
Let's retreat ere it's too late.
Those Secesh will laugh in scorn
When they see that we have gone.

The Charlestonians.
God of mercies! Thee we praise,
Helper of our trying days;
Surely henceforth Thou wilt be
Fortress of our liberty.
No cause is there for despair
While our God is everywhere.

April 1863.

THE WORK OF AN IRONCLAD.

PART FIRST.

April 11, 1861.

' Come, my fair one, sit thee down,
    And sing for me thy sweetest song.'
' Not here; I'm tired of the bright town,
    And of this most vivacious throng;
So rather let us seek the bank
    Of the grand river that I love.
Come where the woods are dark and dank,
    And let thy songstress be a dove.'
Love, nature, youth, in meek decorum blent,
    She hung upon his arm as forth they went,
In pace that longed to fly, but only crawled,
    Like children by an angel's form appalled;
And neither spoke lest both hearts should o'erflow,
    Until they'd gone as far as they could go.
Then Lulie spoke, while Herbert seemed to hear,
    Although he only knew that she was near.

R

' I like to stand upon the verge
  Of the mysterious cypress-swamp ;
Its very gloominess doth urge
  My spirits to a girlish romp.'
Then Herbert looked at her sweet smile and sighed,
  Swallowed a thought and earnestly replied,
' Would I were two men, so as I
  Should never have to leave thy side,
Though for my State I bled and died ! '
  Then Lulie laughed.   ' The boy is mad.'
' Ah, if I were ! Vandals, defiled
  By envy and whate'er is bad,
May yet make Southern women flee
  To swamp like this, and call it home.'
' Herbert, how silly thou can'st be ! '
  ' War hastens.   I can see the foam
Of bitter hate and jealousy.'
  ' Where, dreamer, hast thou been to-day ? '
' Upon my knees in prayer for thee.
  Nay, bright flower, droop not—still be gay ;
I have but thee and liberty.
  Hid now in death's grim skeleton,
She is austere, and chills my heart.
  But thou, my life ! thou art my sun.
How can I live from thee apart ? '
  ' Cheer up ! our freedom will be gained
Without a blow.   Now, dreamer, smile ;
  Smile soon, or I too shall be pained.'
' Not yet ! not yet ! wait but awhile.
  On wintry days before one goes
Into the cold he warms his veins ;
  And I before I meet my foes
Would close my life to deadly pains.
  If I can but be full of thee,
I shall not mind long march or fight.
  I'm sworn to thee and liberty ;
She is so sad, thou must be bright.'

PART SECOND.

April 1863.

An iron monster grimly moves along
The Mississippi, and she sings this song :
' I'm not made to stand fire—not I! not I !
I'm but whip-syllabub.   Let no one try
To test the delicacy of my skin ;
And Lincoln knows that it would be a sin
For any one to think me man-of-war.
No! I am only a triumphal car,
Whose ponderous wheels shall crush free Southern
    States,
Till Hungary and Poland are their mates.
Soldiers must hide their heads when I appear,
Nor rouse my ire, or I'll make towns pay dear.
If any dare presume to fire on me,
I'll burn a town to let the whole world see
That iron monsters were not made to be
Targets for guns.   I'm delicate.   Poor me !
        *   *   *   *   *   *

Herbert was one of many braves who stood
On Mississippi's banks.   A cypress wood
Shielded them from the foe on ironclad ;
And as they waited Herbert grew more sad.
They must attack the boat, nor let it go
Unchecked to work upon their homes dire woe.
But well he knows that cowards are within,
Who dare pronounce all slavery a sin,
But think it brave and honest Christian work
Of conquerors, to burn towns like the Turk,
And ravish women, gloating on the charms
Which they, like devils, hold in fiery arms.

PART THIRD.

Alone, foot-sore, and weary, Lulie crouched
Where a dark cane-brake some protection vouched.

Her father murdered, brothers far away;
Herbert she knew had been in the last fray.
Her sister, worse than dead, she'd fled afar,
Safer with beasts than in a Yankee war.
When morning dawned she thought that she was
    rich;
When evening fell she'd no bed but a ditch.
Her father murdered, that had tried to save
His daughter from a fate worse than the grave.
She thought of him, and said, 'Thank God, he's gone,
And ne'er will know my sister child of scorn!'
While thus she thought, her dog upon her sprang,
And pulled her dress, and then the cane-brake rang
With his loud howl, the while he strove to pull
His mistress forth.   She saw that he was full
Of some mysterious errand, and arose,
Looked out in gathering twilight lest some foes,
When others had embarked, behind remained.
The first thing she perceived—her servant brained
By blow of Yankee gun, she could not doubt:
But she knew not her refuge he'd found out,
And died because to brutes he'd not revealed
The neighbouring ditch where she had lain concealed.
She tried to draw him to a safer place,
But failed, and laid her mantle on his face.
Carlo still howled, and ran on to the bank:
'Herbert is there,' she thought, and, fainting, sank
Upon the ground.   'Had Carlo found him dead!
For all the braves who were alive had fled.'
Some time she lay unconscious of her pain,
Until a well-known voice pierced her cold brain,
And roused her from the swoon; she thought she
    dreamed,
For through the brake a moaning echo seemed
To say, 'Lulie, Lulie, I hope thou art dead!'
Then came a groan.   She heard and raised her head.
'Let her die now, O God! her cup is full.'
She'd almost swooned again, when Carlo's pull

Made her shriek, 'Herbert!' Then the air was still,
Because the heavens took from it its wild thrill.
But her voice had aroused her, and she went
Where Carlo ran : then a low wail she sent
Up to God's throne. HE heard. The maiden fell
Upon her lover's breast and knew no more ;
And the same angel both their spirits bore
Where justice reigns.   Vengeance God vowed to
    wreak
Upon the cowards who protection seek
For iron monsters by fierce demons' deed.
When such can't conquer, ruin is their creed.*

'KENTUCKY, MY MOTHER.'

Kentucky, my mother,
    I lay my heart on thee !
That man is my brother
    Who will fight thee to free.

Kentucky, my mother,
    I feel ev'ry blow
That is levelled at thee
    By ingrate, Southern foe.

Thou hast suffered and bled
    Southern sisters to free ;
And thine own breast is red,
    Pierced by tyrants' decree.

But some scout and hate thee
    Who cannot understand
Any test but success—
    Such Kentucky should brand.

* I suppose I ought to acknowledge the resemblance to the
motto, 'Rule or ruin,' but I am sure I never thought of it. I
wrote the poem at a sitting, thrilling with indignation. Cypress-
swamps and cane-brakes are often side by side, and no one
familiar with the 'sugar-coast' scenery can fail to remember
the universal ditch.

A FRAGMENT.

Matilda. Why need'st thou go away from me, my
    love ?
Thou wilt not fight for home, or lands, but wilt
Leave all to enemies who thirst for it.
    Henry. Thou art a woman, wife, and thou can'st ask
Me to remain in dalliance by thy side,
While Southern brethren battle for their wives!
    M. As precedent that all Kentuckians
Theirs should forsake !
                  H. Ah, Tillie ! tempt me not,
Think what I owe to thee ; but now
Be brave, and bid me fight for liberty.
    M. That I may live in lonely slavery.
    H. Come in, Therese ; your visit's opportune.
Come, help me to persuade my wife to yield
Consent.
           M. For him to shield children and wives
Of other men, and to forsake his own.
    Therese. One word suffices for all argument—
Butler's a word which all pure women loathe.
    M. I shudder, but yield not.   Who's to protect
Me when such monsters come into our State ?
    T. Our God.
            M. Then let Him shield the women of
The South.
    H. Dear wife, I never thought I'd have to blush
For sentiment of thine.
           T. A woman who
Loves well prizes the honor of the one
Beloved, far, far above her happiness.
    M. (*Blushing.*) But Henry will no honor gain on
    field
Where he may bleed.   Look at our neighbourhood ;
There's scarce a family but has a son

Or dear one in the South, yet Southrons curse
Our State.   One thing I've noticed oft : those who
Defend their own are called brave men ; those who
Forsake their own to mind the business of
Some other men no credit get.   If this
Were not so I would bid my husband go.
But if he falls Kentucky loses one
Son more, but gains no honor by his death ;
His children gain no fame, but will be cursed
By those for whom their father died.
Those who Kentucky curse brand all her sons ;
So if my children can't have heritage
Of fame, let them have competence, nor be
Reduced to poverty for sake of those
Who scorn all those who less than they endure :
Forgetting that they suffer for themselves,
But we for them.
                    T. You're selfish, Tillie, now.
  M. You say I'm selfish.   From the South I learned
To think more of my State than other States.
To me the thirteen were but as one land,
Till its abuse and alienation from
Mine own taught me the saddest lesson I
Have learned—we are not one.
                              H. But we will be.
Kentuckians will fall in ev'ry field.
  M. As they have fallen from the first, to die
Unnoticed, and unhonored, and alone.
  H. And from their blood will spring in time to come
More gratitude and love for those who could
Have stood aloof, and yet rushed South to die.
  M. (*With scornful laugh.*) No, never will men
        who have left their homes,
Forsaken wife and child, dared beggary,
Exile and death, be counted equals of
The men who are obliged to fight to save
Their property and lives.   A patriot
Is one who loves the land that gave him birth,

And her defends.   Were the South quite
As noble as I used to claim she was,
Kentucky would be honored for her sons,
The many thousands * who've left all to fight
For liberty of those who scorn them still;
Pitied she'd be for handful of base men
Who, backed by Northern bayonets, control
Her destinies.
        H. She ought not to have been
Deceived into a fatal sleep.
        M. Nor would
Have been had not the Southern Government
Said, 'Feign to be asleep.'
        H. She slept, indeed,
And cannot now be wakened easily.

TO THE GOVERNOR OF OHIO.

Dedicated to Lieut. T. Bullitt, 2nd Regiment Kentucky Cavalry.

Brig.-Gen. Morgan, and many of his officers, through whose veins courses the best blood of Kentucky, were immured in the Ohio Penitentiary, because their daring valor had so often half crazed that State.   Governor Tod offered the penitentiary to Burnside.

Put them in a convict's cell!
   That's the worst that you can do!
Do it! 'twill be grand to tell
   Afric's despots; they have you
Henceforth as authority,
   For their lawlessness can't do
Much that here they may not see.
   Turkish Pasha might envy you.
Put them in a convict's cell!
   Ages hence 'twill be a shrine
Where greyheads will children tell
   Of the old and savage time

* Not half of them known as Kentuckians. They were in almost every regiment.

When the men who nobly dared
  Independence to proclaim
In a convict's dungeon fared
  With criminals!—not theirs the shame!

Bind them tight with convict's chains,
  Since the lust of gain hath crazed
Brothers' hearts, and wise men's brains.
  Their cruelty hath oft amazed
Men who scorn the Northmen's plea,
  That so gracious is their sway,
All must have their liberty,
  Though some loathe much to obey.
COME, BROKEN HEARTS, whose loves are in the ground!
Here's one whose life is bound
To a cold form that sleeps in a fresh grave.
Ah! I am but a slave,
Lashed by a heavy, strong, electric chain,
Which gnaws my life in twain.

Come, broken hearts, whose heroes martyrs are!
My love dwells in a star
In fame's high galaxy—fame warms me not.
No: I ne'er did allot
To him a seat in any sphere so far
From me as a cold star.
But never did death ask me how I'd choose
My precious one to lose;
Yet if he had to go, for freedom it
Was best to die.   I sit
Alone.   I would not mind if I could share
His mansion fair.
But I must wait so long; death will not fly
To me because I lie
In dumb despair, bound to the lonely grave
Of one I'd die to save.
To save from what? from happiness and God?
I, not he, feel the rod.

BRIG.-GEN. JOHN H. MORGAN IN A PENITENTIARY !

Hide him in a dark cell,
  And fame will crown him there !
But know, no place is dim
  Where noble spirits bear
Chains forged by jealousy,
  Weighted by petty spite.
Thus in antiquity
  Those who did strive for right,
Condemned by fear and hate,
  For their greatness suffered.
Such history avenged,
  And centuries have heard
Their praise rehearsed by bards
  Who scourged their cruel foes.
Such will be Morgan's fate,
  Greater for his great woes.
But all of the base men,
  Made baser by their fear,
Who treat him savagely
  History's scorn will sear.

AN ENIGMA.

My whole forms a part of what means 'no one knows ;'
My second's a name given oft to my foes ;
My third is a vowel which often is mute ;
My fourth is the name of a man of repute ;
And syllable last you plainly can see
When you pick up a book, whatever it be.

Why are the prisoners at Johnson's Island like Puck?

MY MOTHER CHURCH.

My Mother Church, on thee I call!
Although my home in ruins fall,
And leave the life, once bright with bliss,
A ruin where hate's serpents hiss;
If thou wilt hear the words I plead,
Although as patriot I bleed,
As Christian I will still be strong,
Believing love will conquer wrong.
I have no home, my Church, but thee,
Where, from man's venom, I may flee.
Thou'st shut thy door on envy's tongue;
Love's banner on thy walls is hung:
There may I shield my aching heart
From best-belovèd doomed to part.
In war's mist fades sunshine of wealth;
To tears and sleeplessness yields health.
My darling one in prison lies,
His heart all torture* well defies;
But I, who cannot strike a blow
To wrest him from a savage foe,
Have no resource but with my God.
Spare him, O Christ! I'll bear Thy rod;
But what if, when I went to pray,
Fanatic turned my steps away,
Trying a wounded heart to probe,
Dishonoring his sacred robe,
Which he doth wear as sign that he
Assumes Christ's follower to be?
Thou, Mother, did'st raise thy voice high,
Said'st that such did his God defy;
Bid him fanatics' meetings seek
His histrionic words to speak;
Nor hurt thy name, thy fair fame stain,
By branding thee with mark of Cain.

* Prisoners of war were tortured in the vile penitentiary at Columbia, Ohio.

TO GENERAL BEAUREGARD.

Rouse thee, my sad hero! rouse thee now to the fray !
In the Yankee ranks scatter wild fear and dismay,
For a tower of strength is thy name, Beauregard,
Rouse thee quickly, my hero, keep sentry's ward.
When this fierce war is over there'll be enough time
To indulge private sorrows ; but now it's a crime
To dwell on our own griefs when dear freedom still
      bleeds,
And women are victims to fanatics' fierce creeds.
Pray rouse thee, my hero ! poor Kentucky now calls
On thee to help ; save her, for fresh terror appals.
Of her long-slighted woes think ! So callous her
      friends,
She is desolate left while her heroes she sends
To fight for the sisters who misjudge her and scorn—
O Beauregard ! hear her, for, like thee, she's
      forlorn.
Her heart is torn from her, a lone widow is she,
More lonely, my hero, than thou ever can'st be.
Thou hast not given sons to die for thee in vain,
Nor hast opened a proud heart to those who disdain
Thy fond love and thy prayers and thy life-crushing
      pain.
Oh, rouse thee, my hero ! for though earth hath no
      mate
For a spirit that's harrowed and tortured by fate,
Wed thyself to thy country, forgetting thy woes,*
For thy grief there'll be time when no more foreign
      foes

---

* I have been told that Gen. Beauregard was so crushed by
the loss of his wife that he refused all offers of command
tendered to him by government. To be my hero one must be a
man as well as a warrior.

Press the soil now made sacred by blood of our dead.
Oh, rouse thee, my hero ! long enough hast thou fed
On sweet pleasures long passed from the sad earth
  away :
They'll bloom for thee again, and will then bloom for
  aye.

DURING A SNOW STORM.

Mist of beauty fills the air
With splendor rare ;
Seemeth earth the clouds to wear.
That fir-tree fair
Shapes its wings like a sea-gull
  Clad in foam-white.
Only my heart is grim and dull
  In its own night.
Ev'ry spray of ev'ry tree
  Glanceth up fair ;
But I nourish gloomily
  Love without prayer.

Oh ! the wind flies merrily
  Through the pleased snow,
But it can't now talk to me ;
  Too far below
Wind and snow hath sunk my heart,
  And in the glee
And gleams of earth I've no part.
  Naught can I see,
When from the windows I look,
  But barren mound.
Then I turn off to a book ;
  For grief hath wound
My brain to its tensest strain,
  And well I know
How much I can bear of pain ;
  I'm used to woe !

Ah ! there is a bird's sweet strain !
   Hath it a nest
That it sings such glad refrain
   With spring-like zest ?
No ; not yet hath it a nest ;
   But it can trust
That it will have one when best.
   In the snow-dust
What could it do with a brood
   Of open beaks ?
Ah, my heart ! Birds will intrude
   Where no man speaks.
Thou'lt have in heaven love and child.
   If they were here
Thou would'st feel thy heart defiled
   By those most dear.
For thou art no traitor, heart ;
   Nor could they be.
They from thee would have to part
   For liberty.
But in heaven they now find
   Freedom and peace.
'Twas thy God left these behind !
   Thy fretting cease.

GENERAL LEE.

I've tried to write of General Lee,
But always stop to bend my knee
For him—God's pledge of victory.
And so I cannot write of him ;
His name makes my best verse look dim.
Then I give thanks or pray for him.

'BLUE COATS ARE OVER THE BORDER.'

Inscribed to Captain Mitchell.

Air — 'Blue Bonnets are over the Border.'

(The old song suggested this; a few lines are borrowed from it.)

Kentucky's banner spreads
Its folds above our heads ;
We are already famous in story.
Mount and make ready then,
Brave Duke and all his men ;
Fight for our homes and Kentucky's old glory.
Chorus.
March ! march ! brave Duke and all his men !
Haste, brave boys, now quickly march forward in
order !
March ! march ! ye men of old Kentuck !
The horrid blue coats are over the border.

Morgan's men have great fame,
There is much in a name ;
Ours must shine to-day as it ever has shone !
As it shines o'er our dead,
Who for freedom have bled :
The foe for their deaths have now got to atone.
Chorus.—March ! march ! brave Duke and all his
men, &c.

Some of us Yanks once caught
The barbarians sought
To destroy our spirit in cold cells of stone ;
But the savages failed,
For not one spirit quailed ;
Now their baseness Buckeyes to us must atone.
Chorus.—March ! march ! brave Duke and all his
men, &c.

The Corn State is ready :
Take aim, boys ! be steady.
Another Butler may come to Kentucky.
        Fight for our lovely wives,
        Fight for our children's lives,
Fight for our homes and our grandsires so hoary.
    Chorus.—March ! march ! brave Duke and all his
        men, &c.

        Fair maidens are weeping
        For those in death sleeping ;
They have no protector unless we can save
        From a strong, wily foe.
        Quick ! to battle we go
To win for the fair the defence that they crave.
    Chorus.—March ! march ! brave Duke and all his
        men, &c.

        Pining for merry play,
        Children* chide our delay ;
Wasting in prison are many brave women.
        We go to set them free,
        Oh, sweet is liberty !
Now over the border let's drive the Yanks again !
    Chorus.—March ! march ! brave Duke and all his
        men, &c.

[Somewhat altered by Editor. General Duke succeeded
            General Morgan in 1864.]

* This word is not inserted for effect. At one time over
twenty children were in the prison at Louisville because their
mothers were. I have heard of two boys, prisoners of war
before they entered their teens. Against the latter I say nothing,
but who believes it necessary that numbers of mothers must be
imprisoned, or the Union be lost !

WAITING FOR A BATTLE.

As one oppressed who feels the coming of
A storm, insensible to splendor of
The glowing sun, darkens her room and tries
To read that so she may, perchance, receive
The good that she is too oppressed to think
Of giving forth ; but fails in this, and yields
To the sweet calm of drowsiness (offspring
Of great excitement and a wearied brain)
That shuts all terror out ; so wait I for
The clash of the armed foreigner, with those
We love who now are coming home to take
Again their own.   My mind in torpor falls.
I am oppressed—but not with terror—no !
A woman of the South, I glory in
Venturous rising of our half-armed men
With an on-crowding foe.   My woman's heart
Is strong to suffer and to break in cause
Of freedom and of right.   I cannot fight ;
But all my days are interrupted prayers.

HURRAH FOR THE RED AND WHITE.
A PROPHECY FOR 1865.

Red, emblematic of love, and white of purity, are the colors of
Kentucky.

Air—' Oh, whistle and I'll come to you, my lad.'

Hurrah for the Red and White, boys, hurrah !
Kentucky has leaped, boys, right into the war.
Her banner has drooped, boys ; but it will no more,
For now it floats proudly an army before.

Chorus.

Hurrah for the Red and White, boys, hurrah!
The Red shows how loving Kentucky hearts are;
The White shows their truth in peace and in war.
Hurrah for the Red and White, boys, hurrah!

The Yankees can boast scarce a lass or a lad; *
So though a few old folk may go raving mad,
With hands in their pockets and heads under feet
Of foreign invaders, young hearts, enthralled, beat.
    Chorus.—Hurrah for the Red and White, boys,
        hurrah, &c.

The South can't upbraid us that we did defer
To hurl back the foreigner, waiting for her
To send us the men and the guns that we gave:
The old State is cautious no less than she's brave.
    Chorus.—Hurrah for the Red and White, boys,
        hurrah, &c.

We men love our wives, and our children are dear.
O chivalrous South! say was it a strange fear
That if in the war, unprepared, we should go
We might have to leave those we love to the foe?
    Chorus.—Hurrah for the Red and White, boys,
        hurrah, &c.

If you on the Border had children and wives,
Oh, how would you relish a midnight surprise—
No weapons in hand, and fierce foe at your door,
And ev'ry by-path made slippery with gore?
    Chorus.—Hurrah for the Red and White, boys,
        hurrah, &c.

But give us the signal that aid is at hand,
And ere long invaders shall seek their own land.

  * I don't believe I have six young acquaintances who are
Lincolnites.

Our hearts have been breaking for many long days;
We're weary of waiting, and sick of delays.
 Chorus.—Hurrah for the Red and White, boys,
  hurrah, &c.

The banner that floated o'er Mexican fields
Proclaimed to the world that Kentucky ne'er yields.*
It never has been trampled on by a foe—
And where that flag waves there the bravest men go.
 Chorus.—Hurrah for the Red and White, boys,
  hurrah, &c.

THE DEATH OF GEN. A. S. JOHNSTON.

As there is no poem in honor of him (one of the greatest of
our generals) among the preceding, the Editor thinks fit to insert
one which has fallen into his hands.

A nation tolls his requiem;
Bring forth the victor's diadem,
  And place it on his bier.
For freedom he threw off his life;
She smiled in victory on the strife—
  But not without a tear.

His life a willing sacrifice
Was offered, and our hero dies.
  In love and sorrow dumb,
The mourning heroes gather round;
His death makes Shiloh hallowed ground.
  How oft will patriots come

To lay a wreath upon the place
Where heroism won the race,
  And despotism flagged
A moment in its mad career,
To ask if more such would appear,
  Ere freedom could be gagged!

* At the battle of Buena Vista Gen. Taylor, watching a
Kentucky regiment, cried out, 'Hurrah for old Kentuck! that's
the way to do it.'

s 2

Then from a thousand voices rose
An answer which declared how glows
   Man's honor for the brave.
Yes, despotism, many more
Their life-blood will as freely pour
   To win a Johnston's grave.

For ages hence 'twill be a shrine
Where hearts will haste when they repine
   Under oppression's bane.
And here they will feel satisfied
'Tis well to die as Johnston died,
   If they his fame may gain.

PATRIOTISM OR LOVE?

For fear the song 'Come away, Love,' may wound one whom
the Editor would grieve to offend, he adds a touching poem,
written by a young lady (as stanch a Southerner as himself) to
one who was engaged to a United States officer.   How the
Editor got the poem is nobody's business but his and the
writer's—it is *confiscated*.

Like child tossed on the waves in scorn,
Without a compass, I float on
My experience (narrow plank !
For some parts of my life are blank),
Looking in vain for hidden pearl,
Striving to read heart of a girl.
Loves she so well that it would be
No sin to give up what to me
Is worthy agony of heart ?
Should she from her loved country part
Now, when true men are casting down
Lives to win the patriot's crown ?

I know that love's a holy thing,
Nor dare I chilling words to fling
At any heart that loves aright,
Whether its fortune's dark or bright.

Is loyalty to country first ?
Or treachery to love the worst ?
A heart *may* mourn its country's woe
E'en while it weds that country's foe.
Must father, mother, be forgot ?
Brotherless be the wife's sad lot ?
But is the one friend worth all this—
Home, country, all that has been bliss ?

Dear one, if you love well enough
To bear friends' taunts, the world's rebuff;
If in the hour of want, or woe,
You'll feel ' 'tis better to be so,
Because I am his cherished wife,
Than to have all the joys of life,'
Then do not change the outcast's lot
To be a queen where he is not ;
If such your love, go bravely on,
Nor hearken to the jeers and scorn
Of those who love their country best :
Enough, if you one life have blest.
Then in the hour when friends recede
From death-glazed eyes, recite your creed.
We are God's children, nor need fear,
Though we part here, 'tis to meet there.

But if such love your heart knows not,
Draw back, nor risk the exile's lot,
Lest all your future life should prove
That only fancies your heart move.
Can he for whom you give up all
Suffice you, when harsh blows will fall
Upon your life ?   Will *your* love bloom
And render sweet an exile's doom ?
His love for *you* cannot suffice.
Beware, lest fancy you entice
To make of self a holocaust,
And cross the life God hath not crossed.

www.ingramcontent.com/pod-product-compliance
Lightning Source LLC
Chambersburg PA
CBHW060617030726
47498CB00005B/1707